# When Vows Are

# Broken

# When Vows Are Broken

*Samuel L. Hair*

www.urbanbooks.net

Urban Books, LLC
97 N18th Street
Wyandanch, NY 11798

ISBN 13: 978-1-60162-390-4
ISBN 10: 1-60162-390-9

First Trade Paperback Printing August 2013
Printed in the United States of America

10 9 8 7 6 5 4 3 2

Distributed by Kensington Publishing Corp.
Submit Wholesale Orders to:
Kensington Publishing Corp.
C/O Penguin Group (USA) Inc.
Attention: Order Processing
405 Murray Hill Parkway
East Rutherford, NJ 07073-2316
Phone: 1-800-526-0275
Fax: 1-800-227-9604

# Chapter 1

## *In the Beginning*

Daryl and April had grown up on the same street. They attended the same schools from elementary through high school. They had been girlfriend and boyfriend since fifth grade.

Daryl joined the military immediately after high school, while April continued living with her parents. She took a part-time job at Target and enrolled at Compton Community College, taking classes toward a bachelor's degree in sociology while patiently and faithfully waiting for her husband-to-be to come home in a few years. The plan was for Daryl to marry her, and work on building a family, a big family. For some reason April had envisioned a large family of four daughters, four sons, and a house full of grandchildren.

Because April and Daryl were madly in love the separation had been difficult for both of them, but keeping their meticulously planned futures in mind and embracing the motto "the best is yet to come," they were determined to endure the long years of suffering.

They had planned to raise their family in a big, beautiful home, with the money he would receive under the G.I. bill. By then she would have her degree and would be making a decent salary, enabling her to contribute to the household finances and, at the same time, save toward their kids' future and education. They had carefully covered all bases. The way they saw it, nothing would obstruct them. "Ain't no stopping us now."

They wrote love letters to one another practically every night during that separation until Daryl was deployed to the Philippines for a tour of duty. Unfortunately, he couldn't resist the young, attractive, ready, willing, and able-to-sexually satisfy Philippine women who came in abundance for a cheap and affordable price.

Soldiers were always their best customers. Some soldiers fell in love and even made arrangements to bring women back to the States after their tour of duty; while others, like Daryl, who had girlfriends or wives back at home, were only looking to blow off a little steam to pass time. Out of curiosity and trying to get in where he fit in, his sex-capades triggered him to begin using cocaine and marijuana, and drinking alcohol at a level of self-destruction. He labeled it as fun but the reality and consequence of it was ruin.

During training camp in Okinawa, Japan, Daryl bragged to his friends and brothers back in the barracks that he had met Japanese women who fucked him like a black woman and sucked him like a white girl. He boasted that he'd even gotten his toes sucked and licked for five extra dollars.

These were the women who possessed the ability to have military men calling home to tell their wives they wanted a divorce, or were never coming back home. There were some men who never bothered calling home.

Daryl and his buddies often competed to see who could have sex with the most women, but Daryl had lost count after number 219. Unluckily for him, he had caught STDs on seven separate occasions from seven different women. Doctors had made it clear to him that he was now unfortunately a syphilis carrier, and that the disease would be a part of him, like an arm or a leg, for his rest of his life. That was something he would take to his grave without telling anyone. No way on earth could he ever tell April about that.

Daryl's letters had obviously slowed down as his transition to becoming a habitual liar, a sex addict, and a disease carrier began.

He was so efficient at whatever he did, in three years he became buck sergeant and was in charge of a squad of eleven men, sharpshooters of various races who literally hated his guts due to his harsh and insensitive way of giving orders.

The times that Daryl had come home on leave, April could not help but notice his dramatically changed attitude. No longer did Daryl open car doors for April or shower her with flowers and chocolates or say nice things to her. And what really devastated her was that the "love by mail" had come to a disappointing halt. *His letters were all I had to cling to until he came home,* she said to herself.

She noticed that he no longer possessed a sense of humor and actually he barely smiled. His demeanor had transformed to an uncompromising authoritative figure that was equivalent to a deranged lunatic at times. But through all of that, April tried to remain positive. *The Army has changed him,* she would say to herself. *But I still love him with all my heart. He's my first, my last, my everything. And we're gonna have a big family, a big, pretty home, and so much love between us, people will be jealous.*

Out of love, April overlooked her fiancé's flaws and embraced the good times they had shared during their school years, as well as their future plans, which was fuel to keep her motivated and sane.

She discovered that she was infected with syphilis after he had returned to his post. Having experienced his new attitude she was reluctant to bring it to his attention, but this was something that had to be discussed, immediately, and not through the form of a letter. She put in an emergency call to his post the following day.

"Shit happens," he said to her, as if it were nothing. Then he began to justify his actions.

"Listen; I was drunk and let a few Oriental bitches suck my dick for a few bucks, okay? No fuckin' big deal! You know where my heart is, baby, and if you ever start doubting where it is, then you've got a problem. You're my trophy wife, my queen, my everything, sweetheart. I love you, April, and nothing can ever change that, not even a disease. So get treated; get over it."

April couldn't believe what she was hearing. She still loved Daryl with all of her heart and soul. She couldn't believe he was talking to her like that.

"We'll put this shit behind us," Daryl continued. "That is, if you plan to move forward with me! Listen, April; those bitches fucked me and sucked me, I ain't gonna deny that, but you're the woman I love and that's all that matters. Get over it!"

She was beyond hurt but, still, she was determined to have his baby. The failed pregnancy test she'd taken each time he left had only saddened her sensitive heart even more.

She cried continually and did not go to school for three whole weeks until finally receiving a letter. Even though Daryl didn't have too much to say in the letter, it still gave her a sliver of hope. It read:

I'll always love you no matter what. Thanks for your support and ongoing understanding. And guess what, sweetheart, I can already hear the wedding bells. Take

care, stay focused, and keep my side of the bed warm
but unoccupied.
   Your First Love,
   Daryl

She noticed he had never apologized for his actions,
but in spite of that, she returned to school the following
morning.

# Chapter 2

## *For the World to See*

When his tour of duty was finally over, Daryl came home and, as planned, he and April were married. They had a big, beautiful ceremony with lots of guests. As time went on, they worked the plan. Daryl had gotten hired on with the Post Office and as time went on he bought them a big house, which they filled with the best things that money could buy.

To friends, family, and just about everybody who knew them, April and Daryl seemed like the happiest couple alive. But behind closed doors, that was far from the truth. When Daryl came home from the Army, his habits of drinking, drugs, and womanizing came home with him. There were many nights when Daryl would stay out all night, if he came home at all. There were days and nights when April sat alone wondering where her husband was and wishing that he would come home. Many a night, she sat by the phone, dialing and redialing Daryl's cell number. He would never answer and never bothered to return her calls.

When he would finally come home, Daryl was met by an angry and frustrated April with questions. Where have you been? What were you doing? Why couldn't you answer the phone or return my calls?

But her questions were met by anger and attitude, as if she had no business asking. And if she continued to ask too many questions, the back of Daryl's hand was the answer April received.

April was enduring a life of occasional physical abuse. There were many days she would go to work wearing sunglasses when makeup alone couldn't hide the black eye. But more often Daryl's abuse was verbal. His brand of verbal abuse was cruel and scared her soul. Although Daryl's verbal abuse didn't leave black eyes or visible bruises, it was causing serious damage to April's self-image.

As April began to internalize the criticism and believe it was valid, her self-image sank lower and lower. She started feeling worthless, incompetent, and unlovable. April felt that if Daryl was thinking that she was so worthless and unlovable, then it must be true.

But Daryl was quite sensitive to outsiders finding out about the abuse, and was very careful to save those scenes for the home, or when they were alone. In public, Daryl was a delightful and charming man. He treated April with such respect that people often called them "the perfect couple."

That's how it was when they celebrated their anniversary the year before. They hosted a party and invited their parents and a few friends. Naturally, Daryl was on his best behavior, laughing and joking with their guests, and he was so loving to April. She silently wished she was married to that man all the time, not just when company was over.

Daryl was very careful to save his cruelty for a private audience of one: April. And like many women, April would never discuss verbal abuse with anybody. So she suffered alone and in silence.

When it came time to open their gifts, Daryl sat with his arm around April as their friends, Chris and Regina Jenkins, gave them their gift.

"We wanted to get you something that would fit the two of you," Chris said. He had known Daryl since they went to high school together.

"Something you didn't already have," Regina added. Although she couldn't really explain why, Regina didn't really like Daryl. She simply put up with him on occasions like this.

Regina handed the gift to April. She smiled and was careful while opening the wrapping paper.

"It's only paper, April," Daryl said and laughed a little. Although he didn't say it, April knew that she was taking too long to open the gift.

She quickly ripped open the paper and opened the box. April removed the contents and showed them to everybody. "They are king and queen of hearts matching lounging shorts," Regina said.

"Oh, thank you," April said.

Daryl grabbed his and stood up. "We are gonna be so cute in these, honey," he said and laughed as he held the outfit up in front of him.

As things quieted down a bit, Daryl's parents, Felton and Brenda Bradford, stepped up with their gift. "Regina is right. It is so hard to shop for you two, because you got everything," Brenda said and handed the present to Daryl.

"That's 'cause my boy knows how to take care of his woman. Just like his old man," Felton said and Brenda took a playful swing at him.

Daryl opened the gift and quickly handed it to April. "It's a knife set for cheese lovers; Pottery Barn antique-silver cheese knives," she said.

"Thanks, Mom, Dad," Daryl said and kissed April on the cheek.

"Yes, yes, thank you," April said. "'Vintage silverware that's been passed down for generations inspired these heirloom-quality knives,'" she said, reading off the box. "'Hand crafted of stainless steel with the names of four types of cheese on the handles.'" April got up and gave her mother-in-law a kiss. "Thank you, Brenda."

"I know how you love your cheese," she said.

When Daryl heard that his mother had bought the gift mainly for April, his eyes narrowed. "Like a little rat," he said and then he laughed.

The next gift came from April's parents, Stanley and Kathy Mitchell. "It's so big," April said.

"Not in front of company." Daryl laughed.

April laughed a little and kept opening her parents' gift.

"It's a mirror jewelry organizer," April said and Daryl rolled his eyes.

"It says it keeps up to three hundred and fifty jewelry items in view while you're dressing and hides them behind the gently tilting mirror when you're set to go," Kathy announced.

The doorbell rang and Daryl got up to answer the door. He opened the door and smiled when he saw it was Anna Sims. Daryl winked at her and stepped aside to let her in. "Hey, everybody, I'm sorry I'm late."

"Let me take your coat," Daryl said.

"That's okay, I can manage," Anna said.

"Where's Harvey?" Regina asked.

"It's just me tonight, Regina. And it will be from now on. Me and Harvey are getting a divorce," Anna said and quickly glanced at Daryl.

"Oh, I'm sorry," April said.

"I'm not," Anna said and handed her gift to April. "It's nothing big," she said, looking at the jewelry organizer. "Just a personalized keepsake photo clock."

"It's got a 'forever yours' picture frame and a clock."

"To celebrate a love that stands the test of time," Anna said and she and Daryl exchanged glances. Their affair was in full effect; only April was unaware of it at this time. But Daryl was the reason that Anna and Harvey had broken up.

Maxine Parker saw the way that Anna and Daryl were looking at each other and she didn't like it. Even though she was married and her husband, Darnell, was sitting right next to her at the time, she was jealous. Unknown to April, she too had been sharing her bed with Daryl. The idea that he was fucking Anna Sims made her want to jump up from her seat and kick her ass, but she knew that she had better keep it to herself. *No point in blowing a good thing,* she thought. Maxine bit her tongue and picked up the gift that they had got for the Bradfords.

"Natural teak wood salad serving set," April said and could tell that Daryl was getting angrier that none of the gifts seemed to be for him.

The only person at the party who didn't have a gift was Tyrone Whitsey. He was a long-time friend of Daryl's who had recently moved in with the Bradfords when his mother put him out.

He didn't have a gift to give, mainly because he didn't have a job, which was one of the reasons why his mother put him out. She hoped that forcing him out into the real world would bring about an acknowledgment that he had to work and become a contributing member of society in order to survive. But all Tyrone did was find someplace else to live free.

Tyrone had only lived with Daryl and April for a short time, but in that time he observed how Daryl mistreated April. He wondered how Daryl could treat her the way he did. Tyrone had always thought that April was beautiful. Now that he lived in the same house with her, he was able to get to know April. He found her to be intelligent and funny. April was kind to him, and considerate, and he enjoyed being with her when Daryl wasn't around.

Since he didn't have a gift to give, Tyrone had told April that he wasn't going to be at the party, that he would find someplace to hang out, and asked if she would call him when the party was over so he could come home. April told him that he didn't need a gift, that if anybody asked she would tell them that Tyrone had given his gift earlier.

It was things like that that made Tyrone wonder how Daryl could treat such a wonderful, considerate, and beautiful woman like April so badly. The more time he spent with her every day, in every way, Tyrone found that he was falling in love with April.

# Chapter 3

## *New Love*

April Mitchell-Bradford was a gorgeous and energetic coffee-with-cream-complexioned African American woman. She had long black hair and a winning smile, and she had the capacity to brighten up any room that she entered. One thing was certain: everybody who knew her loved her. *Everybody but Daryl,* she thought. As her husband, he should love her most of all. But that wasn't the case.

April rubbed her hands over her stomach, anticipating the joy of the first time she would hold her baby in her arms. She paced back and forth, trying to figure out how to tell her husband not only about her affair with his best friend, Tyrone, but also that she was pregnant by him.

After he was kicked out of his mama's house, she and Daryl allowed Tyrone to move in with them.

At first, with Daryl being gone all the time, she and Tyrone became friends. Tyrone listened to her problems and concerns, unlike her husband. They laughed together, watched movies together; they danced to oldies, and played cards and dominoes. And then one day, it happened. They were talking and all of a sudden there was silence. One second April and Tyrone were looking at each other, and the next they were kissing.

Now April was pregnant with the baby of another man who she was undoubtedly in love with. She wondered how she would tell Daryl. She knew that she had to choose the right time to deliver the news, because Daryl could be violent if you caught him at the wrong time.

Suddenly, Daryl walked through the front door. He stood six foot five, and was controlling and narcissistic. She could deal with that, but Daryl cheated on her relentlessly and not just with one woman. He had been unfaithful for years and with many different women. Now he didn't even bother to try to hide it.

It was no longer a secret to April or anyone else for that matter that Daryl had been with Anna Sims. She had become his favorite. The two indulged in drugs, alcohol, and hot, freaky sex, which was something he could not convince April to do.

Daryl walked in the house without acknowledging April. He walked right past her and made his way to the bathroom.

Daryl had an attitude, as he usually did when coming home to April after being out with Anna. Sex with her was incredible. Now he was ready to take a long, hot shower and then he wanted to go to sleep. Anna had that effect on him. He could tell by looking at her that April wanted to say something to him, but he didn't want to hear any of her usual shit; not that night, or any other night for that matter.

Since Daryl was well known for his hot temper, April knew better than to just rush in there and start talking, especially with what she had to say. With that thought in mind, April gave her husband time to enjoy his shower and a few minutes to settle in afterward before she approached him. When she thought that enough time had passed, April collected herself, and calmly but cautiously approached him. Typically, April held her head down low and tried not to make eye contact with him when she talked. But not that night. This was the time to be courageous, unashamed, and deliberate.

"I need to talk to you about something, Daryl," April said, having gathered a large dose of courage.

"Then talk," he replied as he prepared his uniform for the following day's work at the post office. He never bothered to look in her direction.

"There ain't no easy way to say this so . . ."

"Just say what you gotta say and quit bothering me," Daryl said and finally faced her.

"I been having an affair. And there's something else; I'm pregnant, too," April said quickly and waited for the burst of anger she knew was coming.

"What!" he snapped.

"I'm sorry it happened the way it did, but—"

"Hold the fuck up, bitch!" he yelled, cutting her off before she could finish. "Slow your roll and put your got-damn brakes on!" He got up and took aggressive steps closer to her.

April could feel the anger and instinctively backed away.

"So what you tryin' to tell me is that you been fuckin' somebody else and got pregnant by him? For real! Seriously?" He chuckled in an attempt to hide the anger he felt at hearing some shit like that coming out of April's mouth. Still, there was a part of him that was not convinced that she was being truthful.

"Bitch, please; I ain't got time for this shit. You got over a million miles on your pussy. Don't nobody want that abused, million-mile-ass pussy!" Daryl laughed nervously and then continued.

"I got that pussy wide as the Pacific Ocean. Why you think I ain't been hittin' it? No walls, no goddamn bottom. Us men like tight pussy. Oh, loose-ass, bottomless pussy, yeah, whatever."

He laughed at his own comment and hoped she would stop this shit. There was a part of him that still wanted to believe that she was just saying all of this to get a rise out of him.

"That's really what you think?" she replied confidently; but at the same time she felt a bit uneasy about the comment. She wondered if Tyrone felt that way. She wondered if he really enjoyed it like he said he did, or if he was just pretending he did.

"You of all people should know that shit happens when vows are broken. But keep in mind that you made me do it, Daryl! Time has proven that you're nothing more than a devil. Humph; the devil I know."

# Chapter 4

## *Prelude to a Murder*

"The devil I know, yes, the master of deceit, a wolf in sheep's clothing is who I fell in love with, and who's too fucking arrogant to accept the truth! In the beginning, I thought you were heaven-sent, but time proved you were sent straight from the pits of hell! But like I said, Daryl, when vows are broken, shit happens. As a matter of fact, a domino effect of shit happens, so strap on your seat belt."

Her reply caught him off-guard and Daryl took a good look at her face. He could tell that she was serious about what she was saying. He stood in silence and looked at April for a few moments before he said anything.

"So what you sayin'?" he finally asked with an attitude.

"I already said it. What part of 'I'm havin' an affair and I'm pregnant' don't you understand?"

"You bullshittin', right?" he said, hoping she'd laugh it off and admit that she was lying. He wasn't in the mood for this. Anna had been full of energy that night, challenging the Viagra he had taken with gusto, but unfortunately she was no match for the man of steel.

"I'm not lyin', Daryl. I can't make it any clearer than I already have; I'm fuckin' somebody else and I'm pregnant, and you already know it's not yours."

He gave her a killer look.

"No shit? You ain't lyin' are you? Okay, then; who is the muthafucka?"

"Does it matter?"

Not in the mood for bullshit, Daryl clinched his fist and took steps toward April. Only this time, she didn't back away.

"Hell yeah, it matters! Now tell me who you been fuckin'! If I gotta ask you again, I'm gon' slap the taste outta your mouth!"

"Since you insist on knowing, it's Tyrone," she said, and stood there with an attitude, trying to be tough.

"Tyrone who, bitch?"

"Your friend, Tyrone. The Tyrone who lives here, that Tyrone," she shouted.

Her courage was rapidly building, as her playa-playa husband stood open-mouthed and silent, and not believing his ears.

"Tyrone listens to me and understands me. While you're out fucking around with those bitches in the streets, he's the one who's there for me! And, oh, he showed me the naked pictures of Anna you sent him, but I ain't worried about it! Keep on doin' you, Daryl, because I'm damn sho gon' keep on doin' me! I shoulda been doin' me a long time ago, but no, my dumb ass sat around hopin' and prayin' that your self-serving ass would get right. I shoulda known better!"

It was so difficult for the controlling, conniving, dirty asshole of a husband to fathom her words that they had him standing there, biting his lip, not knowing how to respond. He wanted to believe she was lying and just trying to get back at him for all the wrong he'd done before and during the course of their depressing and not-meant-to-be marriage.

He chuckled, trying to conceal his anger at April. "You just fuckin' with my head, right?"

"You can't handle the truth, can you? Accept it, Daryl, because I'm not just fucking with your head, okay?"

Having been with April since elementary school, he sensed her sincerity and frowned.

"Did he take the pussy or what?"

"No, he didn't."

"So you just gave him the pussy, right? Is that how it went down?"

"It wasn't just about sex, Daryl. Our relationship is and has been based on emotions, sincerity, understanding, and attentiveness. Substances you do not possess."

"Relationship! Ain't that a bitch!" Say it ain't so, bitch, say it ain't so!" he furiously yelled. "What the fuck did I do to deserve my wife and friend fuckin' behind my back? I know I ain't been a saint, but gotdamn, bitch, I ain't neva' fucked one-a your friends! How low can you go, bitch?"

"You yuck-mouth piece of shit, you've done much worse than that, Daryl."

"How?

"Are you kidding me? For real, Daryl? What wrongs have you done to me? Is that your question, Daryl? Well, let me see; you've been cheatin' on me for God knows how long. Not that that justifies what I did, but anyway, you lie every time your lips move; you gave me STDs not once, but twice. And not only did you stay out all got-damn night on several occasions, two, three, and even four days at a time, but I'll never forget the time when you came home with lipstick on the front of your underwear. But what really gets me, Daryl, is that you're too damn arrogant and heartless to apologize for any and every got-damn thing you did! I hate you for that, Daryl, and I'm certain that my feelings will not change toward you, ever!"

"Whoo-pee shit!" he replied. "Don't even try to come at a strong nigga with some weak shit like that! I should slap the taste outta your mouth, bitch!" He pointed a finger in her face. "Anyway, back to the matter at hand. I know you gettin' an abortion, right?"

April frowned. *He actually had the audacity to ask me to outright kill my baby because he couldn't produce kids?*

"Hell no, I ain't gettin' no damn abortion and kill my baby! I'm keepin' my baby! And fuck what you goin' through, Daryl. You started this shit, so be man enough to accept the consequences."

"You ain't gon' disgrace me, or shame my last name havin' a got-damn bastard baby. Do you understand me, bitch?"

She held up her hand and shoved it in Daryl's face. "Talk to the hand and kiss my ass, Daryl. I'm keeping my baby and that's not debatable!"

He grabbed her and slapped her hard in the face. She was stunned a few moments, but quickly regained strength and courage and grabbed the fireplace poker and held it in striking position.

"Muthafucka, if you eva', I mean eva', put your fuckin' hands on me again, I'll kill you!" she cried. April was filled with emotion and rapidly building anger.

"You ain't gon' kill a fly, bitch, so quit foolin' yourself!"

"Hit me again, muthafucka, and see what happens!"

Sensing her seriousness, he changed subjects. "I gave you everything you wanted and needed, regardless of what I was doin' in the streets! I took care of you! I—"

She cut him off before he could finish. "Material things! Seriously, Daryl? You tried to pacify me with material shit when I wanted you and needed you, your time, attention, your love and support, but what I got was a bunch of demands and other bullshit I didn't deserve! Lord knows I tried to make things work between us. One heartbreak led to another! You never listened to me, Daryl; it was always about you! Your way or the highway as you put it!"

She caught her breath and continued. "Yeah, I fucked Tyrone, and it was good, too. And guess what, his dick is way bigger and better than yours. He knows how to make me cum, unlike your selfish ass! Maybe if you weren't so got-damn controlling and stubborn, and at least tried to make things work between us then, maybe, it wouldn't have ever happened! Ever since you got out the military, you've been a monster. You've been yellin' at me like I'm one of your troops, instead of talking to me like I was your wife. You abused me emotionally, verbally, and physically, and I'm fed up with all that, Daryl. You gotta man up and take some of the blame too!"

He nodded in disgust, frowning. "How could you stoop as low as fuckin' my friend I let move here? That broke muthafucka ain't worked a day in his life, and lived with his mama all his goddamn life, and your stupid ass go and fuck him and get pregnant by him! I don't believe this shit! But you know what; I can't blame him, 'cause a man gon' be a man, especially when some easy pussy is in his path."

He silenced himself a moment. "Hold the fuck up; so you sayin' you was fuckin' him while I was at work, and fuckin' him in the bed I bought, right?"

"That's what I'm sayin'," April said, then copped an attitude. "Now you hold the fuck up! I put up with your shit all these years because I loved you, regardless of how you treated me! I wanted to have your baby, Daryl, but your selfish, stubborn ass refused to leave those got-damn drugs and street bitches alone and follow the doctor's orders to bring your dead, useless sperm back to life! You gave me a black eye, twice, had me going to work wearing dark shades tryin' to cover it up, but people ain't as stupid as you think they are! You socked me in the mouth and knocked my tooth out, and afterward took me to the dentist to get it capped, but the emotional scar you left on me, Daryl, can't be disguised like the tooth can! Like I said, I put up with your shit for too damn long. But you know what, Daryl, I'm not heartless, or unforgiving like you. I'm sorry for what I did, but—"

He charged at her. "I know you a sorry muthafucka, bitch, and I'm 'bout beat your snake ass to death!"

She swung the poker at him, aiming to hit a homerun but missed, allowing him to grab it and wrestle it away from her. Then he slapped her repeatedly and slung her to the floor. He then tried kicking her in the stomach, in an attempt to kill the baby, but the good Lord provided her with strength enough to block his kicks and cover her stomach, protecting her baby.

"You can beat me all you want, but I'm keeping my baby," she yelled.

He continued beating her like a madman, and then suddenly had a better idea to finish her off.

# Chapter 5

## *Murder*

The 911 call came in at seven-thirty that evening.

"Somebody broke in my house and shot my wife in the bathtub! I think she's dead! Blood is every-got-damn-where!" Daryl hysterically said to the dispatcher. "Get some help over here right got-damn now! Send the fuckin' ambulance to 1012 South Castlegate right got-damn now!"

Outside the Bradford house, Anthony Hicks struggled to calm Daryl's vicious barking dog and to try to keep him from bursting through the gate.

The dispatcher managed to remain calm and keep her composure. "Okay, sweetie," she said in a Southern voice. "Just stay on the phone with me until help arrives, okay?"

Daryl said nothing, but could be heard crying. The dispatcher assured him that an ambulance was also on the way. At the same time Daryl cried into the phone and listened to the 911 dispatcher, Anthony Hicks wrestled with the gate, fighting to keep the vicious dog from breaking through, actually fearing for his own safety.

Neighbors began coming out of their houses and noticing something strange was going on in their usually quiet neighborhood. Anqui Heming, the nosiest neighbor on the block, brought her vehicle to a halt and jumped out as if she were a reporter. She was wondering why Anthony Hicks was fighting with the gate. *Why wasn't Daryl outside when his vehicle was there?* Anqui thought.

"What's goin' on?" Anqui nosily asked. She was the type who would always try to give advice to others on how to live, and how to clean up their backyard, when her backyard was overly filthy.

"I think somebody broke in," Anthony Hicks replied, still fighting with the gate. "I'm tryin' to keep this gotdamn dog from gettin' out!"

"Where's April and Daryl?" She was determined to get to the root of things.

Another neighbor emerged and began asking questions. "Where is Daryl and April?"

"I don't know where April is," Anthony replied. "But Daryl just went in the house." Anthony then told them his wife was calling 911.

Even though Anqui had no idea what was going on, for some reason she saw this as her chance to imitate her mentors, Rachael Maddow, Katie Couric, Anderson Cooper, Reverend Al Sharpton, and the legendary Larry King. She would report the story to a reputable news anchor and sell it to the highest bidder. This definitely was her big shot. She had already begun practicing asking the "hard questions." She would soon have her degree in journalism, and soon after would be ready for the big time and spotlights, anchoring the big stuff. Her failed attempts to find out what was happening did not deter her persistence.

Seconds later, Sherry, Anthony's wife, appeared, holding a cordless phone. She had just hung up from calling 911, reporting a burglary at the Bradford residence.

"Call Daryl's house and see if he answers," Anthony suggested, while an eager Anqui agreed with him.

"I called there about ten times but the phone just rang, rang, rang, and nobody answered."

Since Bruno, the dog, had always been better with her than with Anthony, Sherry offered to take over the gate. Anthony agreed, and Sherry held the gate and began talking to Bruno, attempting to calm the dog. It worked, and Anthony ran around the front of the house to see if he could see Daryl. Just then, a police SUV pulled up in front of the Bradford home.

Sergeant Whitsey, a veteran of the Compton Police Department, stepped out of his vehicle, grabbing his revolver. The athletically built, corrupt sergeant had been on the force many years, and despite being charged with taking drugs, money, and Rolex watches and other valuables from various people, he still managed to hang on to his position. Also, he had been accused by several women of forcing them to give him a head job or pussy, and not paying his tab.

The sergeant was a lady's man without question; he smiled when speaking, he was noticeably handsome. He had short, curly hair, a pair of tight Mitchell eyes, and a pair of dimples that caused most women to go into a momentary trance at first acquaintance.

Seconds later, a sheriff vehicle arrived, this one with a female officer, Angela Stevenson, appearing like she was a full-time member of LA Fitness. A Compton-bred dime-piece who had grown up on Stevenson Street in the heart of Compton, Officer Stevenson was medium brown complexioned, and possessed an onion butt and a teasing pair of titties, standing proudly, refusing to go unnoticed.

Officer Stevenson walked swiftly from her car to join Sergeant Whitsey to be brought up to speed on the situation. The sheriff's department covered several sectors of Compton and often, due to jurisdiction, worked with Compton police in such matters, even though neither institution was enthused about it.

The initial report was a burglary, but during the drive to the house, Sergeant Whitsey had been notified that the incident had been upgraded to a murder. According to the dispatcher, a woman inside the house had been shot in the head.

"Who's in there?" Sergeant Whitsey asked Anthony Hicks, while clinging to his revolver.

"The man who lives here, Mr. Daryl Bradford," Anthony replied, and then began giving more details.

Anthony shadowed Sergeant Whitsey and Stevenson as they made their way around the house to where Sherry held the gate. When they told her to, Sherry let go and stepped back, prompting Sergeant Whitsey and Officer Stevenson to approach the gate. Almost as a reflex, they slammed it shut as Bruno once again charged the gate, barking viciously, baring his teeth.

"A Rottweiler," Stevenson said, knowing the breed to be fierce. Yet she and Sergeant Whitsey knew that they had to move quickly because someone inside the house was injured. Bruno snarled and barked, protecting his territory from the intruders, as they discussed what to do. All the while, the dog pounded against the gate, the latch so loose Sergeant Whitsey and Stevenson pushed to hold it shut.

Anqui approached the officer, wanting answers, and almost demanding them right then. "What's goin' on?" she asked, pad and pencil in hand.

The contemptuous sergeant gave her a defining look that she quickly understood as "buzz the hell off!"

Anqui's persistence, presence, and annoyance triggered Sergeant Whitsey to lash out at her in a not-so-respectful manner. "Are you a reporter or just a got-damn—"

Stevenson cut him off before he could finish, having sensed he was about to say something sarcastic and heartless, as he typically did whenever circumstances caused them to meet again. "This area is off-limits, ma'am," Officer Stevenson said.

Anqui pushed forward her agenda. No way in hell was she going to allow these simple-ass police officers to screw up her possible one big shot at becoming reputable. "I need to know what the hell is goin' on!" Anqui insisted, not taking no for an answer. "I live on this street and have a right to know!"

Whitsey and Stevenson looked at one another, nodded in disgust, and ignored the nosy neighbor. Shouting above the harsh-barking dog, Stevenson and Whitsey discussed alternatives. Deputy Stevenson drew her weapon and held a sniper aim at the ferocious dog.

"I think I'm gon' have to lay his ass down," she said. "A hot one to the head will calm it."

"We gotta do what we gotta do," Whitsey said.

Quickly they agreed they had no other options. Someone was injured, and there might be an intruder. If the Rottweiler wouldn't let them pass, they had to shoot it. Whitsey gave her the nod and Stevenson closed an eye, preparing to enter the yard and do what she had to do. If the dog attacked, Stevenson would shoot it in self-defense. Then, as she opened the gate, Daryl appeared in a white T-shirt and a pair of sweatpants, opened the back door, and walked out of the house.

"That's Daryl right there," Anthony said.

Anqui eased up close enough to get an earful, and luckily the officers, trying to find out what was going on, didn't say anything to her.

"Secure your dog, sir, before we kill 'im!"

As ordered, Daryl called the dog, then grabbed Bruno's collar and walked it into the garage. With the Rottweiler finally secure, Stevenson and Whitsey entered the backyard.

Daryl appeared hysterical and the first thing he said was, "My wife's dead. What dirty muthafucka would do some shit like this?" He began crying and held down his head as if deeply troubled.

Anqui took notes and wanted to initiate a line of questioning, but didn't want to get thrown out and blow her chances at the possible exclusive. All she had to do was observe, write, and then report.

"Where is she?" Whitsey asked, still clinging to his gun.

"In the bathtub," Daryl replied, only now, all of a sudden, he seemed unaffected by the situation.

Whitsey instructed him to wait with Stevenson while he went inside the house.

For the next few minutes, Stevenson stood on the patio outside the back door with Daryl Bradford, waiting for Whitsey to return. It struck her as peculiar that Daryl didn't look as upset as she would have expected him to. His wife was dead, but Stevenson didn't see any tears in Daryl's eyes. *What kinda husband is he?* Stevenson thought.

Anqui stood by quietly on the patio, waiting with Daryl and Officer Stevenson. She actually wanted to question Daryl, but didn't want to appear too intrusive, which could easily lead to her dismissal.

An ambulance finally arrived as Sergeant Whitsey exited through the back door. Dispatch had told them that there was an injured woman, who was possibly deceased. Whitsey led the medics to the dead body.

"Don't touch anything!" he instructed. "And be careful where you walk. This is a crime scene and we don't need to contaminate it."

"We know the drill, Sergeant," the ambulance tech said as he entered the building. "This ain't our first dance."

They were soon standing in the bathroom, staring at the remains of April Bradford. She lay on her stomach, turned slightly to the side. Her left hand was cocked awkwardly beside her and her right arm was hidden from view beneath her.

The medics saw no need to take her pulse. There was no chance that she could be saved.

Brain matter had splattered everywhere, more so next to April's head and her left hand. The medics realized that the blood had already begun to dry. The medics also realized that from the condition of the body and blood, a lot of time had elapsed between the 911 call and their arrival on the scene. April Bradford was dead.

The would-be rescuers suddenly retraced their steps, back to the door they had entered through, and on out to the yard. Sadness surrounded them. The more experienced medic asked if the woman's husband was on the scene. Whitsey nodded at Daryl sitting in a chair next to Deputy Stevenson, taking his statement.

As a medic, Ellis, questioned Daryl Bradford, Officer Stevenson strung yellow tape across the front of the Bradford house. Once that was done, she guarded the front door, as Sergeant Whitsey called dispatch to notify and navigate detectives to the scene, ASAP.

During that time, Alina Estrada, a neighbor, was cooking dinner, when her kids ran to tell her that the police were at April and Daryl's house. She didn't believe them at first because they lied so damn much, but their persistence and faces defined that they were telling the truth this time. They all walked outside and Alina saw the yellow tape and the police cars. She then

spotted Anqui Heming trying to pry answers out of
Stevenson and Anthony Hicks. She then noticed Daryl
sitting in a chair; head buried in his clasped hands, but
where was April? The kids had told her that an ambulance had come and left without hauling anyone off;
this meant that something had happened to April. *Oh,
my God!*

A shift supervisor had sent Gary Prator, a lieutenant
detective, to the scene. Prator assigned Detective Donald McCaney, who had a reputation for taking over, to
assist him. They had left in individual cars.

Minutes later, another call went out, this one to
Gregory Bonner, a crime scene investigator who was a
few miles closer than Prator and McCaney. Bonner arrived at the scene first.

He joined the department and found he enjoyed the
work of piecing together evidence.

On this night, he arrived at the Bradford residence
and found Sergeant Whitsey, who filled him in on what
he knew about the dead woman in the bathtub. Bonner asked where the husband was. Whitsey pointed at
Daryl, who was still sitting in the chair, head in clasped
hands.

"Put him in a squad car and keep him there for the
moment," Bonner instructed.

Whitsey ordered a nearby officer to escort Daryl to a
police car, and then afterward, he and Bonner began a
walk-through of the crime scene.

Entering the house, Bonner wasn't sure what waited
inside. All he knew was there was a dead woman in the
bathtub, and his job would be to collect evidence to
determine exactly how she had died.

Bonner looked down at April's corpse and all of
the blood. Not wanting to disturb the scene, he and
Whitsey quickly left. Bonner suddenly wondered if the

death could be a suicide and if the woman's body was lying on top of the gun.

Freddy Dennis, a crime scene specialist, was the next to arrive on the scene. He had also grown up in Compton, not too far from the home where Prator was raised. During their years as teenagers, they had both embraced wrongdoing and were wannabe Crips gang members, but were grateful they had decided to go a different route. What really had enticed them was the cool way that gangsters walked and talked, and the intimidating way they carried themselves, and how easy it was for gangsters to get girls. "Good girls are attracted to bad boys," someone had told them.

Thank God, they had both come to the realization that they could not accomplish their dreams and at the same time be members of notorious street gangs such as the Compton Crips. It was either one or the other.

Dennis seemed to be destined for police work, after one day discovering a woman's bullet-filled dead body with a crack pipe in her mouth, behind a Dumpster at Kelly Park. He reported his findings to a dispatcher at 911, and had then told his story to police and detectives. From that day forth his interest in police work, particularly the investigative aspect, had skyrocketed.

Bonner and Whitsey explained the situation to Dennis: a slender, jet-black complexioned African American with short hair and expressive eyes. After the detective and the sergeant explained the situation, Dennis, as the lead CSI officer on the scene, gave instructions.

"Do a gunpowder test on the husband," he said.

Bonner walked across the street to where Daryl Bradford sat, in the back seat of a police car, to do an atomic absorption test for gunshot residue, to determine whether he had fired a weapon. Bonner explained what he was doing and Daryl quickly agreed, holding his hands out to be swabbed.

"Sorry for your loss," Bonner said, wondering if the victim had taken her own life.

"Yeah, thanks, man," Daryl dryly replied. "Guess we all gotta go someday."

After that, Bonner walked away, thinking that for a man who had just lost his wife, Daryl Bradford appeared remarkably calm. And to have responded the way he did, saying, "Guess we all gotta go someday," just wasn't the type of response a man who had just lost his wife would give.

"Could be a suicide," Bonner told Prator.

"Yeah, right," Prator sarcastically replied. "I could smell shit a mile away from here. Somethin' fishy about this, Greg. This shit just doesn't pass the smell test."

Detective Gary Prator was a slender African American, with a light brown complexion and a bald head, and was equipped with street smarts, instinct, and a degree in psychology, which had collectively assisted in elevating him to the top of his game. He'd grown up secretly wanting to be a cop, but because of his environment, he displayed the image of a Compton gangsta/hustler during his teens. When Prator applied, the Compton Police Department needed crime-scene investigators. "What the hell," he'd said to himself. "Why the hell not? If you can't beat them then join them." Luckily, he had not caught any felonies after all the dirt he'd been involved in.

# Chapter 6

## *One Hour Since the Death of April Bradford*

The street was filled with county vehicles, police cars, and unmarked cars. The clock was ticking. Statistics show that homicide cases not cracked within the first forty-eight hours have a high probability of never being solved. They had come to no conclusion as of yet.

Being that the street was flooded with police personnel, Sergeant Whitsey instructed an officer to handle traffic, and commanded another officer to keep the countless neighbors and reporters in order.

A cocky, medium brown-complexioned African American with a low-cut fade haircut, and a pair of beady, sharp, confrontational eyes, Detective McCaney had a mixed reputation in homicide. Some viewed him as overly confrontational with suspects, more likely to try to bully a confession instead of using finesse. He was also viewed as a guy who got the job done by all means necessary. McCaney was medium brown complexioned, clean shaved, and always had a neat appearance—despite his fetish with wearing hip-hop attire and Jordans. He was very outspoken and had no problem telling anyone when he thought they were wrong or guilty of a crime. He was a new addition to homicide, but had been a nineteen-year veteran with the sheriff's office, including a lengthy period as an undercover narcotics agent during those nineteen years. He had been promoted to homicide only nine months earlier. He still walked with the cool swagger he'd adopted in his teens, and still somewhat had the appearance of a thug. His motto when confronting or interviewing someone was "guilty until proven innocent." He was so methodical and determined, lots of his coworkers referred to him as Mr. Obsession.

Most people, both on and off the force, secretly envied McCaney, due to his possessions: a white Lexus, a black Corvette, and an eye-catching, well-kept home located in an upscale, predominately white area. Rumors floated through each department he'd worked in for the past years accusing McCaney, because he was a single man with a thug mentality, that his possessions had come by way of taking large amounts of cash as well as significant amounts of drugs from drug dealers to finance his lavish lifestyle. Unfortunately, they were all dead wrong. It was simply his A-1 credit that rewarded him that way of life. One thing he strongly believed in, unlike his ex-wife and many others, was paying bills on and in most instances before time.

On and off duty, McCaney dressed in designer, hip-hop attire, which most of his coworkers and superiors thought was ridiculous. They kept their thoughts to themselves and dared not say anything derogatory toward him to his face, but of course they discussed him among each other.

McCaney worked out vigorously seven days a week, for his most valued asset, in his mind, was his body. He enjoyed watching detective movies and shows such as *Perry Mason, Matlock, CSI: Miami, New York,* and *Los Angeles,* as well as *Law & Order.* He had a thing about such movies and shows. Other than that, he enjoyed driving his vehicles, showing them off. Fortunately, he had no vices.

As McCaney was being brought up to date on what was known so far, McCaney looked out to the streets and saw the victim's husband talking to two people, an elderly man and woman.

Earlier, Anqui Heming had asked Sergeant Whitsey if she should call Daryl's family. Whitsey had told her no. Anqui, however, ignored the order and decided to notify Daryl's parents anyway, and told them something had happened at Daryl and April's house. She had made it her business to get as many neighbors' telephone numbers as possible years earlier in case of an emergency. The wannabe reporter was more so looking out for her own best interest, hoping to score points toward launching her career change.

Felton and Brenda had rushed to the scene, screeching to a stop in the middle of the street, almost hitting one of the police cars. Running up to their son, they embraced him, but after discovering that April was dead, Brenda began screaming hysterically, while holding her son's hand.

Prator suggested that Whitsey ask Daryl to sign a "consent to search" form, which would give police permission to enter the scene and collect evidence. In the US, the simplest and most common type of warrantless searches are searches based upon consent. No warrant or probable cause is required to perform a search if a person with the proper authority consents to a search. A consent search requires the individual whose person or property is being searched to freely and voluntarily waive his or her Fourth Amendment rights, granting the officer permission to perform the search. The person has the right to refuse consent and, except in limited cases, may revoke consent at any point during the search.

In addition, the prosecution in any trial using the search results as evidence is required to prove that the consent was voluntary and not a result of coercion. However, in contrast to Miranda rights, officers conducting a consent search are not required to warn people of their right to withhold consent in order for consent to be valid. Nor are they required to conduct a search in a way that gives the individual an opportunity to revoke consent.

Prator then explained that he wanted Daryl Bradford kept segregated in the back seat of a police car until they were ready to talk with him. While Whitsey did as requested, Prator turned his attention to Anthony Hicks, to hear firsthand what Daryl's neighbor had witnessed.

Prator interviewed Hicks while Sergeant Whitsey explained the consent to search to Daryl, who had no problem signing it.

Prator had been in homicide for thirteen years. During his upbringing, he was obsessed with watching detective shows like *Columbo, Baretta, Hawaii Five-O, Cannon,* and *Dragnet,* which contributed solely to his career choice and character.

In anticipation of entering the scene, McCaney brought along a pair of gloves. Before he went inside the house to begin his investigation, he was approached by Deputy Angela Stevenson, who told him that Daryl wanted to talk with someone in charge. McCaney walked over to the police car and knelt down. His silent, stern stare convicted Daryl before a word was exchanged.

The sun had set and the streetlights had come on. The evening was cool and McCaney had on his long leather coat, appearing streetish.

Daryl broke the silence, but didn't appreciate Mc-Caney's hard, silent stare of conviction. "How long do I have ta sit in this damn backseat, man?"

McCaney looked at him, sensing he was only interested in what was unfolding around him. "You in a hurry or sumpin?" McCaney sarcastically asked.

"All I'm sayin' is—"

McCaney cut him off before he could finish. "If I was you, homie, I'd watch what the fuck I said, you feel me? Keep in mind that whatever you say can and will be used against you, if it comes down to it. And to tell you the truth, homie, from what I gather shit ain't lookin' too good for you, so my advice to you is to watch what the hell you say, unless you ready to confess."

Daryl snapped, "Fuck you, man! You ain't gotta get smart with me and be treatin' me like a fuckin' suspect!"

McCaney frowned and delivered a hard, verbal jab. "You mean to tell me that your wife has been killed and you ain't even affected by it? Sumpin wrong with that picture, homie. You can't convince me that sumpin ain't wrong with that picture. I think you did it or have knowledge of it; how about that?"

Daryl snapped again. "You don't get paid to think! And like I said at first, you ain't shit!"

"We'll see about that," McCaney replied. "I'll show you what I get paid to do, in a real way, potna. You lucky I'm on duty, because if I wasn't, I would commence to beatin' your guilty ass."

"I'm confident it would be the other way around," Bradford threatened.

"Anyway, I'll tell you one damn thing that's for sure: this murder stinks, and you've got shit all over you. Read between the lines, punk."

Daryl blew a fuse. "You don't talk to me like that, man! Don't you know if people hear you talkin' like that they gon' think I killed my wife, just because they heard you say it?"

"Shut the fuck up," McCaney said. "If you didn't do it then don't worry about it. Anyway, I need to take you down to the station for a thorough interview, that's what I need ta do."

"Why you need ta take me to the station?" Daryl asked. "Somebody broke into my damn house and killed my wife, and you wanna take me down to the station? What part of the game is that?"

McCaney sensed Daryl would play his role to a tee, and had no plans to confess, at least not then. But he knew that at the station, people had the tendency to talk in more detail, which often implicated them one way or another in a crime.

"How many times you been to jail?" McCaney curiously asked, having yet not run an arrest record.

"I ain't never been to jail in my damn life! I'm ex-military. I was a sergeant of a forceful, effective squadron and had people like you beneath me, you get my drift?"

McCaney chuckled. "So this'll be your first time, huh? Most people start in the minor league, Bradford, but a fool like you said 'fuck it,' and decided to hit a homerun yo' first time at bat, huh?"

"Fuck you, man! I'm a government employee as we speak, who has served my country with honor and dignity, and don't deserve to be thrown in the back seat of a got-damn police car for nothin', and damn sure don't deserve to be taken to no fuckin' police station to be interrogated!"

McCaney wasn't at all moved by the comment, but gave Daryl another hard, stare. "I'll tell you exactly what you are," McCaney said, "because I can see right through your deceptive bullshit! I know your kind, Bradford; I'm from the hood too, you feel me? You stand tall and look good wearin' that fuckin' mailman clown suit. To your neighbors, you appear like a up-standing, praiseworthy citizen, camouflaging the piece of shit you really are! But trust me, as this case prog-ress, I'll bet my bank account that evidence or witness-es prove that you're a wife beater and a no-good piece-of-shit liar. Yeah, I know your kind, Bradford. You're a transparent punk and I can see straight through you!"

Daryl lost it. "Fuck you, man!"

McCaney fired back. "We'll see who's the one who gets fucked. Anyway, I need ta know what your wife did today, so we can get to the bottom of this shit. I'll be back, so have your lies in order, potna."

With that, McCaney turned and left. Enough obnox-ious exchanges were made for Daryl to hate the detec-tive's guts.

On the patio, McCaney joined Prator, Bonner, Den-nis, and Whitsey, who had the signed C.O.S. in hand. Whitsey led the way, giving his third tour of the eve-ning, this time to the men who'd be in charge of the investigation.

Through the back door, Whitsey led the detectives to the kitchen instead of toward the den. As they walked through, it appeared to be a typical middle-class home and immaculately kept. Photos were scattered throughout, including on the fridge, depicting Daryl and the woman who lay dead, both smiling, seemingly in high spirits. Or was it just a façade? Had Daryl put the photos in view to paint a picture-perfect marriage?

The men followed Whitsey into the master bedroom and on to the bathroom. They peered in at April's body. It was Prator who decided to initiate the investigation. At one point, while considering the possibility of suicide, he wanted a closer look. He leaned over the body. With a gloved hand, he parted April's hair, getting a clear look at each of the three gunshots.

Prator suddenly spotted a bullet mixed into the brain matter lying next to April's body. He took out his pen and picked up the shell. "It appears that the killer had held a gun to the back of her head and fired."

No longer was there a question of suicide. April Bradford was murdered.

"Just what I thought!" McCaney furiously said. "I'll bet my fuckin' badge that low-life punk husband of hers had sumpin to do with this. I know he did!"

Detective Prator put on gloves and continued his examination of the body. He discovered that there were three entrance wounds in the back of April's head. "We got us a homicide here, boys and girls," Prator announced.

A call was made to the shift commander and the investigation officially became Compton Police Department's case number 66-0900-2177. From that point forward, everything collected, every note taken would be labeled with that title. The detectives now knew they had a homicide scene to process. Starting in the master bedroom and bath, they went slowly through the house, assessing the overall picture.

There was broken glass at the back door, suggesting a burglary, but there were some inconsistencies that challenged that assumption. One of the first things Prator noticed was that a jewelry box and the mirrored jewelry organizer were in plain view, most likely belonging to April. Through the glass top, he could plainly see money and jewelry. They saw no evidence the box had been disturbed. On top of the five-drawer chest was a television. Next to it, Dennis spotted a plate containing a man's watch, wedding ring, and a gold necklace, which most likely belonged to Daryl.

"If a burglar broke in then why didn't he take the jewelry and cash?" Prator commented.

Leaving the bedroom, the investigators deliberately and slowly retraced their steps through the house. On the floor, Dennis pointed out a set of keys.

"That seems odd. Who would leave keys on a floor?" Dennis said and made a mental note to photograph the keys.

The detectives entered the dining room and saw nothing that appeared in disarray. However, someone had apparently opened the drawers, but hadn't rifled through them, looking for valuables. "Why not? If it was a burglar why didn't he take anything?" Bonner questioned.

"You're right," Prator said. "And look at that." He stood, hands in pockets, looking at a television on its side on the floor in front of its stand.

"Well, I'll be damned," McCaney said. "A staged burglary. I knew it, I fuckin' knew it. That muthafucka out there is guilty as sin. Look at this shit; the television is still plugged into the power and cable outlets, ain't this some shit? If someone was gonna steal it, wouldn't they have pulled out the plugs before attempting to carry it off?"

On closer inspection, Prator noticed scrapes on the front of the television stand, where wood had been knocked off. He then spotted splinters on the carpet, as if the damage was fresh. He collected the wood as evidence. To Prator, it didn't appear that someone had tried to pick up the television, but rather wanted to slide it down to the floor.

"Like you said, McCaney, this whole scenario appears to be staged to look like a burglary."

"Damn right it is. Looks like he used the stand as leverage and eased down the television," McCaney injected upon further evaluation. "Like I said, that muthafucka is guilty as sin; I'm tellin' y'all he did it! I see straight through that fake-ass mask! He thinks he got everybody fooled because he's ex-military and now a got-damn mailman, but that's where the deception comes in!"

Despite McCaney's strong assertion of Daryl's guilt, Prator and Bonner were not ready to jump to any sudden conclusions, but based on what was in front of them, things appeared very obvious. They had all had their fair share of jumping to conclusions and being misguided by their imprudent hunches, but at times, such as this one, just couldn't help themselves.

As a result of their reckless and self-guided decisions, their cases went unsolved and the media took pleasure smearing their names, dragging them through the mud, as if they were incompetent and incapable of performing their job duties. They promised to never again jump to conclusions.

This wasn't a scene Bonner and Prator expected to see. Burglars typically ransacked houses, wanting to get in and out quickly, before anyone walks in and surprises them. They usually open drawers and rifle through the contents. One thing they did not do was leave behind easily seen jewelry, cash, or television sets. The dots just weren't connecting.

But relying on his instincts and years of experience, in Detective McCaney's mind he had already deemed Daryl Bradford guilty of murder, without question. He would use the force of his personality to slowly convince the others that his opinions and impulses were correct.

"This shit stinks!" Detective McCaney said.

Prator thoughtfully commented, "Humph. If the door was closed when the window was broken, shouldn't the glass be in front of the door, instead of the den?" Prator said, already knowing the answer.

He looked at Bonner, and all the investigators understood what the others were thinking. The entire scene appeared abnormal. Even the time of day was odd. Burglars rarely struck in late afternoon, when neighbors were busy with families returning from work and school. They also didn't usually carry heavy guns, such as .44 Magnums.

"Now one-a y'all look me in the eye and tell me this shit don't looked staged," McCaney said, frowning, daring any of them to challenge him.

"We're on the same page," Prator replied. "We've investigated hundreds of burglaries, but this one just doesn't add up, and damn sure don't look the way a burglar scene normally looks."

"I smell shit, Detective," McCaney reiterated.

With Daryl outside in the police car, what pieces of the puzzle could he provide them with?

Prator instructed McCaney to stay on the scene while Bonner and Dennis documented and collected the evidence.

"Sergeant Whitsey said he'd take Daryl Bradford in for questioning," Prator then said. "There are lots of unanswered questions and—"

McCaney cut him off. "Let me take that punk in! Give me the honor of questionin' him!"

They all looked at one another. Bonner had heard about McCaney's interrogation tactics and did not agree with them at all. "We're gonna conduct things decently, orderly, and legally, McCaney," Bonner made clear. "I don't like this any more than you do, but we've gotta do things the right way."

"I agree," Dennis added.

McCaney snapped, "Ain't this some shit? So why in the hell am I here then? Y'all don't want me to do my damn job or sumpin? Un-fuckin'-believable!"

Prator walked outside and, following policy, asked Daryl Bradford to go down to the station with him to make a statement, filling in what he knew about April's activities that day. Daryl agreed.

Moments later, McCaney left the crime scene and made his way to the station, craving to inject himself in the interview.

# Chapter 7

## *Two Hours Since the Death of April Bradford*

Meanwhile, Anqui Heming had unsuccessfully attempted to extract information from several police officers, ambulance drivers, and detectives, and since no one offered her anything, she drew her own conclusions based on her observations until eavesdropping, listening to the coroner.

"Incredible," she said, wild-eyed with her mouth open. "This is some juicy, hot shit! CNN, here I come!"

She wasted no time quickly spreading the word that April had been shot in the head three times with a .44 Magnum, and that Daryl was a suspect and was recently hauled off to the police station. She rushed to her vehicle, grabbed her laptop, and carefully jotted down her observations and hearsay in a fabricated and exaggerated manner, hoping to hit a homerun with the story.

Daryl's parents stood by and watched as the police cruiser pulled off, taking their son to the station to be interviewed. They followed in their own car.

Detective Kim Stinson, another of Compton's finest, born and bred in Compton on Stoneacre Avenue, had been promoted to detective after having been a Compton police officer for eleven years. He had been recently promoted to sergeant detective, and had been asked to interview Daryl's parents.

The interview rooms were eight-by-eight white-walled quarters, each equipped with only a table and a few chairs. The prevailing theory of the best way to conduct an interview was to get a drink and use the restroom before starting, then keep the witness or suspect for as long as necessary, up to hours at a time, answering questions. To avoid all distractions, the best setting was a bare, blank room, with nothing to distract.

McCaney had not only successfully inserted himself into the Bradford interview, but had completely taken over the interview at one of the distant substations. Prator allowed the tactful, street-smart detective to do what he did, offered no objections, and decided then to return to the crime scene, where he felt he would be more useful.

Because of his earlier confrontation with the rent-a-cop, Daryl wasn't enthused about McCaney taking over the interview, but he had no choice in the matter.

Daryl, calmly and thoughtfully, still not comfortable talking to McCaney, described those first minutes after he found his wife's body as being in total shock. When you have something that traumatic, one is not capable of putting into words how they actually feel. Sometimes it feels like an eternity and sometimes it goes quick. Some even have trouble walking and some seem to never recover.

As part of his strategy, after discounting Daryl's statement and labeling it as bullshit and deception, McCaney had taken Daryl to the main corridor, and told him to wait on a bench for the time being. His aim was to cause Daryl as much discomfort as possible. Uneasiness sometimes led to confessions.

A rookie deputy was seated nearby in his uniform, working in a cubicle. The deputy said little to McCaney, not wanting to do anything to jeopardize the interview that was about to take place. Another officer pulled the rookie aside, out of Daryl's presence, to enlighten him about the man on the bench. "He's the victim's husband," the officer told the rookie.

As he waited, Daryl looked around with an angry expression; then he suddenly turned to the deputy. "How long you been a cop?" Daryl asked.

"Not too long," the rookie replied.

Daryl sensed the man didn't want to talk to him; therefore, he silenced himself and continued staring at his hands.

Meanwhile, McCaney explained to Detective Stinson that he wanted statements taken from both of Daryl's parents. Although Stinson had only been in homicide a few months, he had been in law enforcement for thirteen years.

Stanley, April's father, had been at the hospital with his father, who was on life support and hadn't heard about the horror unfolding in Compton. Leon, his brother, had called twice, after receiving a call from Anqui, who had tracked down his telephone number in the Yellow Pages, trying to tell his father about April, but could not manage to find the words. When Stanley got on the telephone, Leon instead asked about his grandfather. But now, as Stanley walked toward the room to see his father for what he believed might be the last time, a nurse rushed forward and said, "You have an emergency phone call."

Stanley picked up the phone and heard a familiar voice.

"Stanley, somebody shot April in the head three times and killed her," his sister said.

For a moment, Stanley Mitchell went silent, unable to speak. Then he fell to his knees and cried. His daughter Denise, known as Necie, ran toward him, and for moment could not understand what he was trying to tell her.

# Chapter 8

## *The Investigation of the Crime Scene*

Detectives are taught that in homicide the most likely suspects are those closest to the victim. When they work a case, unless evidence or circumstances suggest otherwise, the most common approach is to first look within a victim's inner circle, at family and close friends. Then, if no solid suspects emerge, they widen the circle, expanding it to include neighbors and coworkers. If there are still no possible suspects, the circle gets even bigger, including acquaintances and strangers.

To eliminate individuals from a list of suspects, investigators weigh multiple factors: physical evidence, possible motives, truthfulness, if an individual is cooperative, and alibis.

As others left for the substation, Prator, Bonner, and the crime scene officer, Dennis, stayed at the scene. Bonner began conducting a preliminary search of Daryl Bradford's garage, inspecting his Tahoe and April's Lexus.

In the back seat of the Tahoe was a Home Depot bag containing a receipt and brackets. Those items didn't strike Bonner as odd at the time; however, he knew that once the Bradfords' activities that night were discovered, they might become meaningful.

Inside the house, Prator and Dennis conducted a methodical search. They first shot a video, preserving on film the way the scene was that night. Rooms where nothing appeared to be out of place were still videoed. The Compton Police Department would have control of the scene for only so long before it would be released to Daryl's custody. Once that happened, there would be no possibility of reconstructing what they found on the night of the murder.

Before they left for the station, Sergeant Whitsey had asked Daryl if there were any weapons in the house. He told them that his .22 pistol was in the master bedroom closet, on top of the shelf.

Dennis grabbed it and laid it on the bed. It was unlikely that it was the murder weapon, so the investigator did not bother dusting it for fingerprints or photographing it. Then he bagged and tagged it to be checked against the shells that they found.

Detective Prator had completed the video of each room. Only when that was done did he and Dennis turn their attention to April's body.

A call had been placed to the medical examiner, Rhonda Cleveland. Cleveland arrived on the scene to inspect the body.

"The main evidence of possible homicide are the holes found in the back of the skull. Three .44-inch inwardly beveling circular holes in the back of her head, which is essentially the description of a .44-caliber gunshot wound," Assistant Medical Examiner Cleveland said as she continued her examination.

"That fits," Prator said. "We recovered what appear to be .44-caliber shells."

Cleveland did not appreciate being interrupted by anyone while giving her assessment. "As close to a perfectly circular hole as you can get in the skull," she continued as if the detective hadn't said a word. "The fact that the hole was inwardly beveling."

"What?" Bonner asked.

She looked up and rolled her eyes. "Bigger on the inside of the skull, Detective; it is also consistent with a gunshot entry wound. High-speed bullets damage organs in ways different from what we usually think."

"How do you mean?" Prator asked.

She took pride in educating the detectives.

"When a bullet travels through the body, it passes kinetic energy to nearby tissue, tossing it out of the bullet's path in a spiral direction, generating a momentary hole, significantly larger than the size of the bullet. The size and shape of the hole can vary," explained the Medical Examiner. She turned over the body. The three shots had entered her head and exited through the front. The damage was catastrophic. Much of the right side of her face, including her eye, had been blown away. Her skull was shattered, her face was distorted, and her mouth was open, as if she had screamed in agony.

Cleveland continued, "The instant consequences of the bullet is bleeding which will cause an insufficient amount of blood to the circulatory system."

Dennis scratched his head and responded, "I always wondered why the exit wound is larger than the entrance wound."

"Exit wounds are larger than entrance wounds because as the bullet travel through the body it slows down and explodes within the tissue surrounding muscle. That is when it has reached the end of its course. This causes the exit wound to look larger and noticeably more devastating than the entrance wound."

As Bonner shot photos before the body was moved, he wondered where the blood spatter had gone.

"A lot of blood," Bonner said.

"Exit wounds will often bleed profusely, as they are larger, but entrance wounds can sometimes look only like small holes; in this case the weapon was fired at close proximity to the victim," Cleveland said.

When he had enough photographs of the body, Cleveland laid out the body bag.

As they would throughout the night, Bonner and Dennis discussed the burglary theory. They'd already documented April's apparently undisturbed jewelry boxes on the bedroom dresser and Daryl's jewelry, including his heavy gold ring, sitting in plain view. On April's corpse, they found more jewelry. Cleveland removed a gold bracelet and necklace, and put them in the envelope. From April's left hand, the physician slid an engagement ring Daryl had given her years earlier.

The black body bag was closed with April's cold, lifeless body inside. Traveling with it to the morgue there would be other evidence. One red plastic bag held brain matter collected from the floor. Another contained shells found near the body, and April's broken prescription glasses.

As they assessed the scene, Bonner and Dennis were puzzled. Once they'd been able to take a good look, they had realized that the shots had almost emptied April's skull.

Bonner took a closer look at the bathtub. It was there that he found what he'd been looking for: the missing brain matter. The tub was covered in blood and tissue.

With this new evidence to consider, Bonner and Dennis discussed the angle of the shots and what they observed on April's body. They had seen dark areas under the skin where blood had settled after death on April's knees and shins. That, coupled with the blood and brain matter splatter, led them to conclusions about her position at the time of the fatal shots.

"She had to have been on her knees in the tub when the shots were fired," Bonner said. "Ain't that some shit."

"Say it ain't so," Prator said. "From the looks of things, the shooter made her get on her knees, where she probably begged for her life. I'll be damned! That is some cold-blooded shit."

# Chapter 9

## *The Interview of Daryl Bradford*

That evening, McCaney and Sergeant Whitsey escorted Daryl to an interrogation room. When detectives or officers interrogate, they want no distractions, no ringing phones, nothing but their questions and the suspect's answers.

Whitsey offered Daryl a drink and the use of the restroom, but Daryl turned him down, irritated by McCaney's hard, convicting, and silent stare.

Whitsey then read Daryl his rights, saying he was entitled to an attorney and warning him that anything he said could potentially be used against him in a court of law.

"We can get this shit over real got-damn fast, homie," McCaney said, pacing the floor. "We don't have to waste each other's time, Bradford, so quit playin' stupid. Keep it real with me and I'll see what I can do for you down the road."

Daryl snapped. "Kiss my ass!" he yelled, then glanced at Whitsey. "Get this fool outta here! I told you I ain't kill my wife! You need ta have your off-base-ass out there lookin' for the person who killed her instead of tryin' to get a confession outta me! For every got-damn second you waste on me, the person who killed her is out there laughin'! And guess what, Mr. Detective; they laughin' at you 'cause you on the wrong damn track, chasin' an innocent man! Now I'm gonna make myself clear and say this one more got-damn time: I did not kill my wife, nor did I conspire to have my wife killed! What part of that don't y'all understand?"

"Good try, potna," McCaney said. "Just not convincin' enough. You're gonna take that lie to your grave, ain't you?"

"Kiss my ass, man. I'm tellin' you I didn't do it," Daryl insisted.

Suspects typically deny accusations; therefore, Whitsey ignored Daryl's comments and asked him to calm down and describe the history of his and April's marriage. As he talked, McCaney looked him over for cuts and scratches. With the broken glass in the back door, it was possible the killer had been injured. Or April could have fought her killer and left scratches behind to help identify him, but McCaney found nothing on Daryl resembling a fresh wound.

Daryl went on to describe his events that day and said that upon returning from a day out of shooting pool and watching a Lakers game at his friend Chris's house after work, he realized something was wrong when he saw the broken window.

After Daryl talked, Sergeant Whitsey typed his statement on an official form and, once finished, ran off a copy and asked Daryl to review it. Daryl said he had stormed inside the house when seeing the broken glass and found April lying naked in the bathtub. He said he walked up to her and shook her briefly, but she didn't move. He said he had checked for a pulse, as the 911 operator asked him to, but didn't find one.

"Like I said, Mr. Detective," Daryl sarcastically said. "You should be out there lookin' for the muthafucka who killed my wife instead of in here fuckin' with me, tryin' to bully a confession."

McCaney nodded and chuckled. "Nigga, please," he said mockingly. "I already told you, I can see straight through you. You might be able to fool the people you surround yourself with, like family and other mutha-fuckas who praise you, but you can't fool me, homie. Been there, done that too many times, you feel me? So lay the cards on the table and stop tryin' to bullshit us and yourself. You got an F for actin'; now come on with the real."

Daryl clenched his fist, frowning, then stood, staring hard at McCaney, who took an aggressive step toward him, triggering Whitsey to jump between them.

"I wish you would," McCaney said, face to face with Bradford. "Make my day, muthafucka, damn I wish you would! Come on, bitch, take a swing so I can lay your ass out! You'd rather swim through a swamp full of alligators and moccasins than to fuck with me, boy."

"Have a seat, Mr. Bradford," Whitsey instructed, holding back an irate Detective McCaney.

Sensing he wasn't going to get anything useful out of Bradford with McCaney's presence, Whitsey suggested McCaney leave the room to calm the air. Suspects sometimes seem to talk when treated well, and appear comfortable talking with a mild-mannered person.

# Chapter 10

## *Meanwhile . . .*

Detective Stinson pulled out his laptop computer and began interviewing Daryl's parents, but each time he directed a question at Daryl's mother, Mr. Bradford would spring up and answer the question for her. That was very frustrating to Stinson.

"Please, sir, don't interrupt," Stinson politely asked the rude man. "This is your wife's statement and it needs to be in her words only. You'll have your opportunity to say what you want to say in your statement."

Obviously, Stinson's words went through one of Mr. Bradford's ears and out the other, because moments later, it happened again. Felton Bradford contradicted Brenda and insisted that Stinson immediately change his wife's words. Throughout the process, Stinson had forgotten that he was the one in charge, not Felton Bradford. In Stinson's estimation, the man was talking down to him, as if he were superior.

Felton Bradford had worked more than a decade as a government official as supervisor in the computer department, setting up classes for county personnel, which obviously skyrocketed his ego. That night, Detective Stinson ran into minor problems using the computer, and more than once, Felton Bradford snapped, "Maybe if you took some classes you'd become efficient with a computer."

The disturbed situation staggered on: Stinson asking questions, Mrs. Bradford answering, and Mr. Bradford impolitely interrupting. Unaware that at the scene suicide had been ruled out, Stinson asked if April had been depressed or experienced hormonal problems, if her death could have been a suicide.

"Oh no," Mrs. Bradford answered, clutching a tissue in her hand. "That's not possible. April was a happy and outgoing person."

"Did your daughter-in-law have any enemies?" the detective asked.

"No. April was liked by everyone," replied Mrs. Bradford.

Then something extraordinary happened. Brenda Bradford buried her face in her hands, and Stinson heard her say in a troubled, mournful voice, "No way could I've raised a son who would have killed his wife."

*There it is,* Stinson thought.

"Mrs. Bradford, I didn't mention anything about your son," Stinson said, about to ask the question, "Why would you think he might have killed his wife?" But he never got the chance. Before he could form the words, Felton Bradford furiously charged toward the desk, chastising Stinson like a parent correcting their teenage kid.

"My wife didn't mean that!" he insisted.

From that point on, Felton stood at attention and on guard, next to his wife.

Stinson angrily excused himself, having to calm down and regroup.

# Chapter 11

## *Back at the Crime Scene*

After the video and photos were finished, Bonner retraced his steps. Then he drew a sketch of the crime scene, marking X's where the broken glass lay; a small amount was in front of the back door, but most of it was on the carpeting in the den. There wasn't any on the blue couch positioned just feet in front of the door. Instead, the glass had scattered to the left of the doorway into the den. Bonner and Dennis inspected the door, not finding any signs that it was damaged except for the glass.

"Simple physics tell me the glass shouldn't be where it is if the door was closed when the glass was broken," Dennis said. "The dots just don't connect."

Once Bonner finished his diagram, he and Dennis bagged evidence, including April's keys found lying on the steps. Bonner then collected the sheets off Daryl and April's bed, and then picked up a blue face towel he found in the bathtub, apparently used by April when showering. As Bonner and Dennis made their way through the bedroom again, they curiously glanced at the undisturbed jewelry boxes.

Dennis had already discovered April's purse in a closet. It seemed an odd place for it. They bagged it and took it in as evidence. Before turning it into the lab, Dennis pulled out an address book and set it aside for the detectives. It consisted of names and phone numbers of friends, who could be potential witnesses.

When the crime scene officers finished in the bedroom, Gary Prator entered wearing latex gloves, observing the scene. He turned his attention to the telephone, photographed it, tested it for fingerprints, and then pressed the redial button. The last call had been made to the Hicks residence: the neighbors. *Why would April call a neighbor rather than 911 if she was fleeing a burglar?* thought a mystified Detective Prator.

Prator then picked up the home telephone next to the bed. He hit redial on that phone as well, and this time 911 answered. Since he knew Daryl had called 911 and there was no record of April calling, that phone, he assumed, was the one Daryl used. As he looked about the room, like Dennis and Bonner had before him, he thought about the undisturbed jewelry boxes and the glass scattered across the den. He and the others had examined and reexamined the door and the glass. The only way they could envision that particular glass pattern was if the door was already open when the windowpane was shattered.

"This just doesn't make any damn sense," Prator said, scratching his head.

Lastly, Prator checked the answering machine, pressing the play button. He listened to the messages Daryl's father and Brenda had left early the prior evening. When finished, he popped the top of the machine open and removed the micro cassette, then slipped it into an evidence envelope, numbered it, and sealed it.

As the investigators worked in the house, it seemed odd. They were in a decent, middle-class neighborhood, processing what appeared to be, from the photos, a happy home. Hidden in the master bedroom but obvious in the bathtub was the horror of what had transpired that afternoon. The puzzle that had to be pieced together was to find April Bradford's killer. Yet much of the house appeared undisturbed.

# Chapter 12

## *Four Hours After the Death of April Bradford*

At the police station, about 9:45 P.M. , tensions were rising.

When McCaney returned to the room, he asked Daryl for more information about his activities that afternoon. Daryl had said that when he had left the house, he had gone to a park to exercise and to collect his thoughts; and, after that, shot a few games of pool and watched a Lakers game at Chris's house. He then gave McCaney the name of stores he said he had gone to: Jack Rabbit Liquor & Jr Market, about seven miles from the house, and Home Depot, located in Long Beach, about thirty miles from his residence.

As they finished filling in the holes, McCaney began pointing out the inconsistencies between Daryl's statement and the physical evidence, from the glass in the den indicating the door was open when the window was broken to the staged look of the crime scene. One big problem with Daryl's story, as the detectives saw it, was the dog. The Rottweiler was furious when defending its territory. Although he knew the animal, Anthony Hicks had been afraid to enter the yard. The dog had snapped and barked, flailing itself against the gate, to get at the officers on the scene.

"This shit ain't makin' a bit of damn sense, Bradford. Deputy Stevenson and Sergeant Whitsey were so got-damned scared of your dog they were ready to kill the muthafucka," McCaney said, staring at the man he'd already deemed as guilty.

"Now explain to me how in the hell an officer couldn't get past that vicious-ass dog, but a got-damn burglar could just walk by it, and do what he wanted to do? The fuckin dots ain't connectin', potna, meaning you're losin' points, and you're that close to losin' the game!"

Daryl didn't respond. Detective McCaney noticed Daryl's aggravated look and continued to press forward for answers.

Throughout the interview, Daryl never looked McCaney in the eye, which obviously was a sign of guilt, in McCaney's mind. Instead, he fidgeted in the chair, displaying discomfort, hesitant with his answers. McCaney judged that Daryl Bradford was nothing more than a stubborn, uncooperative asshole, who actually felt he'd committed the perfect crime. *I'm gonna nail this piece of shit!* McCaney promised himself.

During a break in the interview, McCaney talked with Detective Richard Jackson. McCaney mentioned that Daryl Bradford said he didn't own a .44 Magnum and that there wasn't one found in the house.

"Did you ask his father about that?" Detective Jackson asked.

McCaney said he hadn't, and Jackson said he would personally go and ask Felton Bradford.

A short time later, Jackson returned and talked to McCaney again, this time telling him that Felton Bradford said he took pride practicing at the shooting ranges, and said that he had bought each of his three sons a gun for their twenty-first birthdays.

McCaney wrote in his report that at times Daryl bowed his head as if trying to look upset, but there were none of the usual physical signs of sorrow.

As the interview became increasingly confrontational, Daryl Bradford stopped talking. He didn't ask how the investigation would proceed and didn't express any more urgency for the detectives to find the man who killed April.

As the interview drew to a close, McCaney again told Daryl that he was trying to rule him out (even though Daryl knew the detective was full of shit), to eliminate him from the list of suspects, a psychological game the detective often played. If Daryl wasn't involved in the murder, a quick way to take the spotlight off him was a polygraph. While not admissible in a courtroom, they are used routinely by investigators who believe the tests to be useful in gauging cooperation and truthfulness.

It was then that Daryl became openly defensive, McCaney detected.

"I refuse to take a lie detector test under any circumstances! I want a lawyer right got-damn now! I won't say another word until he's present, so either you let me go or charge me and let me call a got-damn lawyer!" Daryl made clear.

Before they parted, McCaney got in Daryl's face. "Your account of the events don't match the physical evidence, my friend. Just like I said from the beginnin', you did it and you know you did it! You killed your wife in cold blood!" McCaney blatantly said, then left the room.

McCaney then checked in with Stinson and took Felton Bradford's statement himself. Mr. Bradford said that his son and daughter-in-law had a good marriage. He also recalled April stopping by the house that afternoon to pick up Brenda's homemade enchilada casserole.

"She was in a hurry," Felton Bradford said.

By then, others had arrived at the station, including the pastor of the church the Bradfords attended, and family: Brenda's brother and sister and their spouses and children. The main entry was filled with people, and Stinson would remember that night as being "out of control."

After he had the statements recorded, McCaney, along with Stinson, talked to Brenda and Felton Bradford about the situation as it stood that morning. Their son's version of the events did not match the evidence, McCaney explained, and Daryl wasn't cooperating. He had refused the polygraph test.

The Bradfords appeared upset, but seemed to take in the information when McCaney told them, "We can't eliminate your son as a suspect."

Felton assured McCaney they would talk to Daryl and that the following day Daryl would take the lie detector test, that he would do whatever he needed to do to prove his innocence.

At that point, Brenda left for home, and McCaney went into an office to call the district attorney's office.

June Johnson was a Creole-complexioned, petite African American woman, with reddish brown hair and a fiery resolve in the courtroom. Despite her beauty, she was scholarly and extremely cocky, described as a pit bull in a designer suit. She was considered one of the toughest prosecutors in all of Los Angeles County.

McCaney explained the Bradford crime scene, the evidence, and events that had unfolded that night. Johnson listened, asking questions.

"Can I arrest the son of a bitch?" McCaney asked when the prosecutor had heard all the facts.

"No," Johnson replied. "I need more."

"Then what the hell do I need to do?" McCaney angrily asked.

"That's simple; bring me the murder weapon," Johnson replied.

Minutes later, Stinson and McCaney watched as Daryl walked out of the substation with his father. There was nothing they could do to stop him.

McCaney decided to return to the crime scene. Dennis had left, but Prator and Bonner were still there, sniffing through evidence. They discussed what had happened at the substation, including Daryl Bradford's statement. The vast majority of it did not make any sense.

Stinson arrived and could not stop thinking about what Mrs. Bradford had said: *I couldn't have raised a son who would kill his wife.*

"Is the husband a suspect?" Stinson curiously asked.

The others filled him in on what they'd seen: the shots to the back of April's head, and the physical evidence that did not match Daryl's story, from the ferocious dog that wouldn't let a police officer in the house, to the debris of glass indicating the door was open when the glass was broken.

The detective listened, thinking about April executed by someone cold and heartless enough to put a gun to the back of her head and pull the trigger three times. Despite everything he'd seen in his years of law enforcement, Detective Stinson wondered, *Could a husband really do that to his wife?*

# Chapter 13

## *The Defense*

Late that evening, one of Daryl's uncles phoned a criminal defense attorney named Willie Starks, someone the uncle knew since childhood in Compton.

Soon after Daryl arrived at his parents house, Starks made his way there, arriving a little after 1:30 A.M. He talked briefly to Daryl's family, and was then escorted outside, where Daryl sat on a bench with his head buried in his hands.

When it came to Starks's client list, most were relatively low profile. At one point, Starks represented convicted drug dealers, which was how he became so wealthy; but since having his family threatened by a reputable drug dealer he'd promised to "get off" after being paid hundreds of thousands of dollars, and watching his client rot through the legal system and being struck out under California's three-strikes law due to his extensive felony record, Starks decided to do a 180-degree turn in taking on clients.

In the dark and cold backyard that night, Starks asked Daryl's brother, who'd accompanied him, to leave them alone, and then talked to Daryl briefly, telling him that it wasn't a good time to discuss the case fully, but that he didn't want him talking to the police without him from that point forward.

"Don't say anything impulsively," Starks advised. "And don't do anything impulsively." Starks always made that clear to his new clients.

Daryl agreed, but seemed preoccupied. Starks couldn't seem to get him to focus on what he was saying, and he worried that Daryl was not getting the message.

On his way back through the house to leave, the defense attorney listened to Brenda's and Felton's accounts of their encounter with the detectives, saying that McCaney had told them, "You need to get used to the idea that your son killed his wife!"

That sent Starks to the backyard again, this time to ask Daryl if the detectives had accused him of murdering April.

"Yeah, they think I did it," Daryl sadly replied. "In fact, they're convinced that I did it, no matter what the hell I say to 'em, especially after I told 'em I wasn't takin' no got-damn polygraph test."

Starks made arrangements for Daryl to meet him at his Beverly Hills office early the following morning, and then left the house.

Felton Bradford noticed that none of the family slept that night, and also noticed that his son remained stunned, as if still in shock. *Is this a front,* he thought, *or did my son really kill his wife? I don't think he did, and hopefully he didn't, but until this thing plays out, I got his back and will do what I have to do. He's my son.*

Meanwhile, at the post office where Daryl was employed, William Roper, his long-term friend/unit manager sent out an e-mail to all staff employees, despite knowing how the vast majority of employees felt about Daryl. The e-mail read: Give our sympathy to Daryl Bradford. His wife was brutally murdered last night.

There were many whispers at the post office that day, much of it about Daryl, as his coworkers wondered if he was behind his wife's murder, due to his affair with Anna Sims. Many coworkers and associates of Daryl had heard about the murder on the news that morning and on the car radio on the way to work.

Daryl arrived at Willie Starks's seventh-floor office with his parents and brothers. It would seem that the family often did things as a tribe, but the defense attorney asked to talk to his client alone. Behind closed doors, Starks still had a hard time getting Daryl to focus on April's murder.

What Daryl didn't appear worried about was the investigation. He barely seemed interested in anything Starks had to say about what the police might be doing. Still, there were things Starks had to ask. Some defense attorneys don't want to know if a client is innocent or guilty, believing that knowledge can tie their hands in the courtroom. For instance, codes prohibit an attorney from putting a client on the stand if they know he or she will lie.

"I tell my clients," Starks said, "that the only thing I want to do is to keep them out of jail or prison, and during the duration of trial, for their own sake, I encourage them to stay out of trouble and to be mindful of their words and actions. I don't give a damn if they did it or not; that's not my concern. I don't approach a case any differently if my client is Charles Manson as opposed to a first-time petty thief who was caught stealing something from Walmart. I have a moral calling to keep everybody out of cages. Just don't let me be surprised with new evidence gathered by the police that you didn't bother informing me about. I can be very persuasive to any jury." Starks was a man of extremely high confidence, and running for the US Senate.

After an impassioned introduction, out of the blue, curiously, even though he had just said that it did not concern him if his clients were innocent or guilty, Starks asked Daryl if he murdered his wife.

"Hell fuckin' no!" Daryl yelled, snapping at the attorney. "And if you ask me some shit like that again, I'm firin' you before I even hire you!"

The question not only humiliated Daryl, but enraged him as well.

# Chapter 14

## *Autopsy*

At 7:30 that morning, Detective McCaney received a call from the medical examiner's office. April's autopsy was scheduled for nine o'clock. It's not unusual for homicide detectives to attend autopsies, to collect evidence and to hear firsthand the impressions of the physician. McCaney called his partner, Detective Prator, and made arrangements to meet him at the morgue.

When they arrived at the forensic center, the assistant medical examiner, who had conducted the autopsy, told them that April's body had already been examined under ultraviolet lights, searching for fiber evidence.

When they walked into the morgue, April's naked corpse lay on a metal gurney in an autopsy suite, the right side of her face a wide open, bloody, raw hole, caused by the large, forceful bullets. Two bags held other evidence, including brain matter, her broken glasses, and the bullet shells. The clothes she had worn that final day rested on a tray underneath the gurney. Although he had seen much in his years in law enforcement, Gary Prator looked at April's body and felt overwhelmingly sad.

The examiner pointed out bruises on April's knees, consistent with her having been in the position Bonner and Dennis suggested, crouched down, perhaps kneeling at the time of the fatal shots, begging for her life.

The examiner turned the body over and inspected the entrance wounds at the back of her head, concluding that April's murderer had pressed the gun against the left back side of her head and pulled the trigger three times. *Unbelievable,* thought the medical examiner. *What maniac would do something like this?*

When McCaney assessed the wound, he concurred with the examiner's assessment; gunshot residue in the wound suggested to both detectives and the physician that the gun had been flush against April's skull. Envisioning this angered each of them even more. "What would trigger a person to do something like this? This is not the work of a burglar; this is the work of somebody out for revenge," Prator said. "Clearly."

With April's body again on its back, the examiner examined the exit wounds. The damage to April's face was catastrophic. As it entered, the force of the powerful bullets had shattered much of her skull, emptying it and blowing out the right side of her face. Her teeth were still in place, but her jaw was broken.

"The deadly shots shattered the entire cranial cavity, exiting on the right side of her face," explained the examiner. "And one more thing, boys."

"What's that?" McCaney said.

"She was in her second trimester."

"What?" McCaney said.

"She was about five months pregnant," the examiner sadly said.

On her report, she listed her conclusions. First: the path of the blasts was left to right. Second: the cause of death was contact wounds to the head. Based on the size of the wounds, the diameter of the contact area, the murder weapon was without question a .44 Magnum.

The autopsy continued, and Prator stayed with the coroner while McCaney took the elevator to the fifth floor, bringing with him the remains of the shells recovered from the scene and the body.

The morning after the murder turned out to be a hectic one for the detectives on the case. As they finished at the ME's office, a call came in concerning a faxed letter withdrawing consent to search. That meant that the Compton Police Department no longer had permission to process the Castlegate Avenue home, now known as the April Bradford murder scene.

District Attorney June Johnson had already been notified, and she wanted McCaney in her office to help write a search warrant. While within Daryl's rights, withdrawing permission made the prosecutor and investigators look even harder at him.

"I'll bet my badge that low-life son of a bitch did it," McCaney confidently said. "You can trust and believe that before this shit is over with, we're gonna find out he's hidin' a boatload of shit. I feel like beatin' the fuck outta him."

At the DA's office late that same morning, Johnson listened as McCaney detailed the discrepancies between Daryl's statement and the evidence at the scene, including the broken glass and the dog that wouldn't let police enter the yard. The detective thought that perhaps he had enough evidence to hook Daryl up while they continued the investigation, but Johnson wasn't swayed.

"I need concrete and factual evidence," Johnson told him. "Find the murder weapon and we'll have a slam dunk."

The first *Compton Bulletin* article on the murder bore the headline: PREGNANT WOMAN FOUND SHOT TO DEATH IN HER HOME BATHTUB.

The reporter said that Daryl Bradford told police officers and detectives that he had returned home to find the body of his wife, April, in a pool of blood, lying dead in the master bedroom bathtub of their home.

# Chapter 15

## *People Will Talk*

As coworkers of Daryl's watched the morning news in the break room, diverse opinions were formed and concerns voiced about Daryl's character, past actions, hearsay, and his open betrayal with Anna Sims.

"He did it," James, one of the coworkers, said. "It's in him to do something like that. Just look at how he openly flirts with Anna and couldn't give a damn who's looking at him or what others say."

"You really think Daryl did some dirty, low-down shit like that?" David asked, but really he already knew how practically everyone felt about Daryl. Most folks despised him because of his arrogance, his having favor with William, his boss, and more so because he cheated on his wife and treated her like shit the few times April had come to his job.

"Hell yeah, I think he could," James replied, frowning. "Narcissistic people like Daryl think they can do what the hell they want, say what they want to people, and get away with it without nothing said! I hate muthafuckas like that."

Bruce Boyden, another coworker, spoke up. He remembered Daryl from his years as a student at Roosevelt Junior High and Dominguez High School. He revealed stories of Daryl's bullying, violence, and even thug mentality at times that led to various suspensions and being banned from school.

"I been knowin' Daryl for a long time," Bruce explained. "He has always been an asshole; that's his middle name. He played tough guy at an early age and that attitude just stuck with him, you know. But at the same time, before he joined the military, he was the type of man who opened doors for April and spent his last money buyin' her flowers and nice gifts. He'd buy her shoes with matchin' purses, all kinds of shit women like from Victoria's Secret. I mean, he treated her good . . . No, golden and respectfully are better terms for how he treated her. But once that asshole was discharged from the military, he was a total different person; all hell broke loose. I sensed that sometimes, by the way he talked to and commanded April to do things, he thought he was still in the military, bossin' around one of his troops, because he treated her like shit, man. Seriously. Now when it comes to bitches like Anna Sims, he treats her like she's superior, or like she's the goose that lays the fuckin' golden eggs! I'm telling y'all, the military converted Daryl into a got-damn monster and changed his whole attitude." The more Bruce spoke the angrier he grew.

"I think he's bipolar or somethin'," Sidney Chambers injected.

"You got that shit right; Dr. Jekyll, Mr. Hyde at his best," added Melvin Wafer. "That oil-slick piece of shit walks around here like he owns the damn place. Rumor has it that he and Anna fucked in the bathroom during the early morning shift."

"I wouldn't doubt it," said Linda Fellows. "I can't stand that got-damn home breaker! I saw her smiling at my husband one day, and oowwee, y'all just don't know, I wanted to walk up to her and just slap the dog shit outta her! I can't stand that home-wreckin' bitch!"

"I heard worse than that," Melvin said. "Two reliable sources told me he picks up crackhead women, and smoke dope with 'em, and get 'em to give him head. Now I know damn well both my sources ain't lyin' about that."

"I wouldn't doubt it," replied Carl Meriwether. "The muthafucka bragged to me about droppin' his wife off at church on Sundays when they only had one car, and then pickin' up one of his bitches, then fuck 'em in the back seat, and afterward, drop the woman off, grab a half pint of whiskey, then double back to church, park in the lot, and wait for his wife to come out!"

"It takes a bold person to do some shit like that," Constant Young replied.

"Nah, uh-uh," Erie Brown injected. "It takes a stupid muthafucka with a death wish to do some shit like that."

"He bragged to me one time about doin' that stupid shit, too," Dennis Johnson added. "Said he fucks a chick he calls Twenty-four. Said the reason he calls her Twenty-four is because she's twenty-four years old. Said she got some good, tight pussy, though! Said all the women call him the meat man."

"Whatever," injected Douglas Smith. "He lie every time his lips move. The muthafucka told me she was gay and neva' had a dick 'til she had his."

"He's a dirty son of a bitch," Calvin Johnson added. "I tell y'all that much. I know he wasn't lyin' when he told me he takes fuck breaks at his neighbor Maxine Parker's house once a week. He said she got that good-good and he can't resist it. Told me the reason he be tryin' to kill Mrs. Parker's pussy and squirt all in her mouth is because he hate her husband. Said he asked her husband one day to use his got-damn lawnmower and the man told him no. Said nobody tells him no!

Told me he called her husband a few times and told him he was fuckin' his wife, and told him Mrs. Parker be suckin' his dick. Said he called the man a wimp, and asked him what he was gonna do about it. Told me Mr. Parker stood five foot even and nuttin' but a coward, and didn't wanna fight 'em."

"I wouldn't doubt it, 'cause that wyanch ain't nuttin' but a slut anyway!" said Shermaline. "Her husband spoiled the shit outta her but the heffa still can't be faithful! I just don't understand a woman who has a good, working, and responsible husband who buys her any damn thing she wants, but she still insists on fuckin' other men!"

"She is who she is," said Paulette Patterson.

"You got that shit right!" added Etta Jones. "A slut gonna be a slut no matter how good you treat 'em, and a dog is gonna always be a dog no matter how good you treat 'em and what you do for 'em. You can't make a housewife out of a ho: that's the bottom line."

Bruce Boyden scratched his head and spoke up again. "I still can't believe he shot his wife three times in the head. That muthafucka gon' rot in hell if he did do it."

"Guilty until proven innocent, I say," Dennis Johnson shouted. "That's the way the courts do it. Guilty 'til proven innocent, and I doubt if he or a lawyer can prove he's innocent."

"I can't stand that arrogant muthafucka," William Roper said. "Man, my wife came up here to bring me lunch one day, and that shameless bastard eyed her down, I mean, the bastard's eyes were at her titties and ass. I shoulda beat his ass right on the spot, and the only reason I didn't was because I thought about the consequences—the house note wouldn't get paid, my grandkids would be without, my got-damn car would get repossessed—'cause my ass would sho-nuff be in jail."

"And the worst part about it," Jeffery Miller said. "Is that he'd probably be fuckin' her or tryin' to fuck her, knowin' you in jail."

# Chapter 16

## *Searching*

Armed with a search warrant, the work resumed at 1012 South Castlegate Avenue. In the laundry room Bonner collected a shirt. On the front they saw a spot that resembled blood. They then grabbed two Post-it notes off the fridge.

In the master bedroom, Dennis claimed as potential evidence a gray warm-up suit, including the jacket, which had been draped over the back of a chair, just inside the door. The reason it caught his attention was that the matching pants were on the bed, as if Daryl had just taken them off. Then a call was put out to a blood expert, asking him or her to respond to the scene to test for blood evidence that might have been missed.

The crime-scene unit worked together throughout the day. That afternoon, Gregory Bonner and Dennis threw fingerprint powder on the doorknobs, parts of the walls, and much of the back door with the broken glass, hoping to find a clue to identify the killer.

At the morgue, April's fingerprints had been recorded. In the end, the prints found in the house belonged to Daryl and April.

In the garage, Dennis processed the Tahoe and Lexus, taking into evidence the Home Depot bag found inside the Tahoe. At the back door, Bonner saw a pair of tennis shoes on the patio and bagged those as well.

When David Lemon, the male blood expert, showed up late in the afternoon, he sprayed luminol, which is used by criminalists to detect traces of blood at crime scenes. In this test, luminol powder is mixed with hydrogen peroxide and hydroxide in a spray bottle. The luminol solution is sprayed where blood might be found. The iron from the hemoglobin in the blood serves as a catalyst for the chemiluminescence reaction that causes luminol to glow, so a blue glow is produced when the solution is sprayed where there is blood. Only a tiny amount of iron is required to catalyze the reaction. The blue glow lasts for about thirty seconds before it fades, which is enough time to take photographs of the areas so they can be investigated more thoroughly.

Bonner and Dennis went through the house, pinpointing areas to test. The shirt they had bagged in the laundry room tested positive. Bonner asked the blood expert to spray the backs of the mirrored doors on the closet. Although sections of the bathtub glowed when the expert held his light stick in certain places, including the area where April's body had lain, there was no indication that the shot had scattered blood and brain matter in the direction of the killer. How was that, when the gun was held point-blank to April's head? They'd soon find out.

When the blood expert sprayed the luminol in the sinks, the drain glowed. When Dennis dismantled it and removed the trap, the U-shaped pipe below the drain that fills with water, it, too, lit up with luminol exposure. He bagged the pipe to be sent in for more testing.

"You think that the killer got blood on him and then washed it off in this sink, don't you?" Bonner asked.

"I do indeed," Dennis answered as he bagged and tagged the pipe.

As they searched, both Dennis and Bonner knew the importance of the evidence, especially if it turned out that a stranger had broken into the Bradford house and had killed April. Unexplained fingerprints or blood could point to a possible suspect. On the other hand, if Daryl was the killer, they also knew that forensic evidence could be difficult. In domestic homicides, where both victim and killer live in a house, it's not surprising to find their fingerprints and DNA present. It would be more unusual if they didn't leave behind evidence of their presence in the form of fingerprints, hair, fibers, DNA, and blood.

# Chapter 17

## *The 911 Review*

Prator returned to homicide, where he asked for a copy of all the dispatch tapes for the officers who had made the scene the evening before. Afterward, he called the 911 center and asked for tapes of Anthony's and Sherry Hicks's calls. He then picked them up and brought them back to the station, where a group of detectives gathered around, Stinson among them. On the 911 call, they heard Daryl talking to the dispatcher.

The first time they listened, it was hard for the detectives to take it all in, so they played the tape a second time.

"He doesn't sound genuine," Stinson said. "Notice how his voice fluctuates from sobbing to sounding calm."

"And the way that he emphasized that the back-door glass had been broken," Prator added. "It was like he was clearly saying, 'I know you cops are all brainless and don't have degrees, but don't miss this fuckin' glass! This glass along with this scenario is my stay-out-of-jail card! Don't fuck it up!'"

The more they listened to the tape, the less believable it sounded to the investigators.

Afterward, Prator was about to head back out to the scene when his desk phone rang. An angry man's voice shouted through the receiver, saying, "I want y'all to know that that got-damn low-down Daryl Bradford fucked my wife in my own got-damn bed a few times while I was at work. I hope and pray that dirty mutha-fucka goes to prison and get fucked in the ass, then go rot in hell!"

"Is that right?" Detective Prator replied, but at that point he was all ears.

"You damn right it is! I forgave my wife because I love her, but that back-stabbin' son of a bitch neighbor of mines, I ain't gon' lie to ya, I felt like killin' him, especially after he called my house, disrespectin' me!"

"What did he say?" Prator calmly asked.

"The man straight out told me that he was fuckin' my wife," the man explained. "And she was suckin' his dick, and what really fucked me up is she don't even suck my dick! But I know he wasn't lyin', 'cause he described the tattoo on her ass, the one on her stomach, and the ones she got on both her titties. And on top of that, he told me her pussy is bald, and it is bald, so I know he wasn't lyin'. He told me he started fuckin' her after I wouldn't let him use my lawn mower one day he asked me to. Told me she mighta been my wife, but she was his woman whenever he wanted her. Ain't that some shit?"

As the man continued voicing his anger, bringing up hearsay Daryl was rumored to be a part of, Prator listened attentively, and wrote down every word the man said.

"What's your name, sir?"

"My name is Darnell Parker."

"And your wife's name?"

"Her name is Maxine; Maxine Parker."

# Chapter 18

## *The Anna Interview*

Anna Sims and Belinda Remy, shared a town home. After a quick interview with Anna, Prator asked if Anna and Belinda would follow him to the police station for a more thorough interview. The women agreed. Once there, McCaney talked to Belinda, while Prator interviewed Anna in a separate room.

"Have a seat, Miss . . . Mrs.?"

"Technically it's Mrs. Sims. My husband and I aren't together anymore."

"Thank you for agreeing to come down and talk with us, Mrs. Sims."

"No problem. Whatever I can do to help."

"How long have you known the Bradfords?" Detective Prator asked.

"I've know them for years 'cause me and Daryl work together."

"How would you describe your relationship with Daryl Bradford?"

Anna started to answer but then she thought about it. *If I don't tell them, they gonna find out anyway and how will that make me look?* She understood that because of her relationship with Daryl, she could be considered a suspect. Anna knew she needed to be as honest as possible. "We are more than just friends."

"What does that mean, Mrs. Sims?" Prator asked.

"Me and Daryl, um . . ." Anna paused. "We had sex."

"One, twice, regularly?"

"Pretty regularly."

"To your knowledge did Mrs. Bradford know that you and her husband were having sex on a regular basis?"

"I don't think so."

"How would you describe your relationship with Mr. Bradford?"

"It was fun and adventurous, but sometimes it was kind of scary."

"What makes you say that, Mrs. Sims?"

"It was 'cause of his sudden changes in attitude sometimes. He was like Dr. Jekyll and Mr. Hyde sometimes. As long as he had his way he was okay, but if he didn't . . . things could possibly get ugly."

That caught the detective's attention. Now he needed to know more about Daryl Bradford's penchant for violence. "How often did you and Mr. Bradford get together?"

"Almost on a daily basis."

"And when you did get together what would the two of you do?" Prator asked.

"You know," Anna said and smiled, but she was uncomfortable talking to the detective about this.

"No, I don't, Mrs. Sims. That's why I'm asking you."

Anna just looked at him without speaking.

Detective Prator put down his pen. "Look, Mrs. Sims, I hope you realize the position you're in. I mean you sat there and admitted to having a sexual relationship with Daryl Bradford, which in my eyes makes you a suspect in April Bradford's murder."

"I ain't kill nobody, Detective," Anna said quickly.

"Well, then, you need to tell me all about your relationship with Daryl Bradford and everything you know about the murder."

"I don't know nothing about no murder. I ain't even see Daryl that day."

"I thought you said that the two of you hooked up daily?" Prator pressed.

"We do. He was supposed to get with me later that night, but that was before all this went down."

"Okay, Mrs. Sims, tell me what the two of you did when you were together."

Anna took a deep breath. "We'd get together before, during, and after work and we'd have sex," Anna began, and then she paused and looked at the detective.

"Go on, Mrs. Sims."

"Most of the time Daryl would have a little something with him."

"Like what?"

"Some weed or some powder."

"At work too?"

"Sometimes."

"Go on."

"Sometimes he would ask me to do stuff like dress up like a nurse, or he get me to put on a Catwoman or Supergirl outfit he had bought for me. One time he made me put on a police uniform and handcuff him to the bed; then he'd get me to rough him up. On a few occasions he made me whip him."

*This is getting good.* "He even hit you?" Prator asked, prying.

"No. I ain't into that. That was his thing, you know. All I did was fulfill his fantasies."

"You said that he could change on you sometimes; tell me about that."

"He could change from sweet to sour just like that. I remember one night we had just got finished"—Anna paused—"doin' it. And he was holding me, and I asked him if he was going home or was he staying the night and he got real mad and started cursin' at me just like that," Anna said, snapping her finger, stressing her point. "But, overall, he was my baby and he treated me like a queen and respected me, and I cared a whole lot about him."

"Did you love him?"

"Yes, I did love him, and regardless of how this turns out, I'll still love him."

"Do you have any idea who would kill April Bradford?"

"No."

"You know, Mrs. Sims, just like I said, your relationship with Mr. Bradford gave you motive to kill April Bradford; his relationship with you gives him a motive to kill his wife."

"Daryl would not and could not have killed his wife," Anna said to the detective.

"But I do need to know everything you know, in order to proceed with our investigation."

"What do you want to know?" she asked, dumbfounded.

Prator continued, "Did you know that he was married when you started seeing him?"

"Yes, I knew Daryl was married."

"And that didn't bother you?"

"No. I was married at the time that we started seeing each other too."

"He ever talk about leaving his wife?"

"No. He never said anything that suggested he would ever leave his wife."

"How does Mr. Bradford talk about his wife?"

"Daryl never said anything derogatory about April."

When Prator finished typing up her statement, he gave it to her to read:

For close to three years or so, Daryl and I have engaged in sex almost daily, and have also indulged in
drugs together after work. Daryl would often stay at
my place at least two, three nights a week, and most
weekends, and yes, I cared about him, regardless that
he was married.

She then mentioned something that caught the detective's interest: six days before April's murder, she
had told Daryl that she didn't want to continue the
relationship. She said that she sometimes felt guilty
about being "the other woman" and about screwing
someone else's husband, and was ready to call it quits
out of guilt and possibly try to work things out with her
own husband. But hooked like a fish, Daryl refused to
free her up, and told her, "Hell no! You belong to me!"

That was the end of that particular conversation.

While Anna initialed each page and signed the end
of her statement, in another part of the substation,
Belinda Remy felt uneasy. The detectives brought her,
as Anna's roommate, in to provide some additional
context and background information about the affair
between Anna and Daryl Bradford, information that he
knew from experience they wouldn't get out of Anna.

She wanted to tell McCaney what she knew about
Daryl and Anna, but didn't want to be disloyal to her
friend. She was extremely careful about what she said,
meticulously guarding her words when talking to the
detective. *Friends are supposed to trust one another
and be able to take shared secrets to their graves,* she
figured. *That's part of what friends are for.*

As she was leaving, Anna wondered if she had said
too much. Since there was a strict "no fraternization"
policy at her branch of the Post Office, Anna was worried about what would happen if her employer found
out about her and Daryl. On the other hand, she was

certain that her supervisor, William Roper, already
knew because, one, he was Daryl's friend, and number
two, the gossip that went on throughout the post office
was overwhelmingly dramatic, juicy, and often even
detailed: exactly what people wanted to hear.

But would William openly confront and fire her
when she had something to hold over his head? *I don't
think he would,* she quickly thought, thinking about
the orgy William participated in, or the time she'd
busted into the room at work and caught him eating
her cousin's pussy.

On their way home in the car, Anna was upset. Although the detective never came right out and said it,
she got the impression that they thought Daryl did it.

"I can't understand how they could think that Daryl
killed April. They don't know what the hell they're talking about," Anna said. "I mean, he tripped when he was
high, but that doesn't make him a bad person because
he isn't! My Daryl wouldn't kill anybody, especially his
wife!"

"You sure about that, Anna?" Belinda asked. "Especially after the way he acted after you told him you
didn't want to see him no more?"

Anna defended her man despite what others thought.
"It's true, I told Daryl I wanted to call it off with him,
because I met Elmer Aubrey, and Elmer didn't do drugs,
he encouraged me to get clean, he wasn't married, he
had his own house and two cars, and more so. Elmer
cared about me and my well-being. I never even had the
chance to fuck him, because I couldn't keep Daryl out of
my pussy long enough! Now I'm the first to admit that
Daryl say and do some strange shit sometimes, but fuck
what they're talkin' about and fuck what they're goin'
through; Daryl is not a killer, and he didn't kill his wife!"

# Chapter 19

## *10:30 A.M. the Following Day*

All day Stanley and Kathy Mitchell waited with Stanley's sister, Lisa, at her home on Nestor Street in Compton, hoping for some sort of news about funeral arrangements. Neither Daryl or his family ever called. Finally, Stanley and Kathy did call the Bradford house, only to get an answering machine, but Daryl never returned their calls. Now, their daughter was dead, and Daryl never called to ask what they wanted for April's funeral. *Very strange and uncommon,* they thought. Even if Daryl couldn't call for whatever reason, at least somebody in the family could have gotten in touch with them.

"I thought the Bradfords were supposed to be Christians," Kathy said to her agitated husband, who was fed up with the bullshit.

"They ain't no different than the rest of the people in the world who claim to be Christians," Stanley furiously yelled, frowning. April, since birth, had always been Daddy's little girl.

"They lie; they cheat on their got-damn taxes and cheat on their wives! They fool people into believin' that they Christians, but their actions prove they ain't no better than a person in the world who don't believe in God! Felton s'posed ta be a preacher, but Lord knows he's full of shit! Just because he knows a few scriptures he calls himself a preacher. Ain't that some shit! Some folks stupid enough to listen to him, but not me. He be lyin' every got-damn time his lips move; he don't fool me! He ain't God! People like him use the Lord's name to cover up the shit they doin'! Yeah, they gon' go to church, yeah, they gon' do that, to uphold that Christian image! They want folks to look at 'em a certain way: a holier-than-thou way, or a 'He or she is a Christian' way. They don't fool me, Kathy! None of these damn hypocrites fool me! I can see straight through 'em, just like I can see straight through my car windshield. Front-row sinners, that's what the hell they are!

"Now my baby is dead, and these so-called Christian in-laws of ours ain't got the got-damn decency to call us and tell us what the fuck is goin' on! Does that sound like a Christian, Kathy? Do it? You see, that's what I was talkin' 'bout when I said that people words and actions define who they really are! I remember Felton referrin' to hisself as a prayer warrior. Prayer warrior my black ass! Him and his son ain't nuttin' but cowards and hypocrites! That's what those fake-ass Bradfords really are! The only difference between me and Felton is that I'm a confessed sinner and he's a closet sinner who try to look good in front of people.

"Sumpin I thought about, Kathy: how is it that Felton and Brenda claim to be Christians and Daryl is a got-damn atheist? What kinda shit is that, Kathy? I remember my baby tellin' me that boy don't believe in God and he don't pray! I don't understand that shit! But somebody gon' pay for what they did to my baby, yep, somebody gotta pay, trust me, somebody gonna pay! And when I find out who did it, I'll bring my got-damn shotgun to court, walk up in there, and kill the muthafucka in cold blood just like they killed my baby!" Reminiscing about various father/daughter moments he'd spent with April, Stanley begin crying, dropping his head in his hands.

# Chapter 20

## *The Next Morning*

Detectives Bonner and Dennis returned to the crime scene later that next morning. The Lexus and Tahoe had been towed to the impound to be more closely inspected. Put in to evidence from the Tahoe was the Home Depot bag with the shelf brackets, and put into evidence from the Lexus was April's cell phone and car charger.

They stood looking at the den television. They had already picked up and placed in evidence the splinters of wood that appeared to have been knocked off when the television was slid down off the stand and onto its side on the floor. Dennis suggested they put the television back on the stand and turn it on. What that might tell them was how roughly the set had been handled.

"How so?" Bonner asked.

"Was it dropped after the alleged burglar had already killed her?" Dennis replied.

"You thinking that he panicked and decided to leave it?" Bonner asked.

"Or maybe he had someone put it down gently, so as not to damage it? If so, it seemed logical that it was someone who planned to use it in the future and didn't want to ruin it. That could only be one person, if that's what evidence shows," explained the wise detective.

"I know what you're thinking," Bonner said. "You're thinking that Bradford eased the TV off on its side so it wouldn't be damaged 'cause after all this is over, he was gonna use it."

"Absolutely. Now your brain is clicking on all cylinders. So far, that's what evidence shows," Dennis said.

Bonner chuckled. "I thought we weren't jumping to conclusions. Anyway, even if it was a burglar, would the same logic apply? Would they want to handle the set with care 'cause a TV that don't work ain't worth nothing?"

"I see your point."

"Still a good idea to look at it," Bonner said.

Dennis and Bonner lifted the television and replaced it on the wooden stand.

"Well, I'll be got-damned," Dennis said, shaking his head. "The damn thing plays like new."

Bonner walked away shaking his head too, as he walked to the back door. He stood there looking at the broken window and thinking about how some of his colleagues had already convicted Daryl Bradford of his wife's murder and were ready to move on the execution. Bonner refused to make that kind of judgment without an in-depth review of the evidence. He agreed the burglary appeared to be staged, but he wasn't convinced that Daryl Bradford set it up.

He crouched down and looked at the door closely. There wasn't much clearance under that door, and he wondered, if the door was opened while the glass was on the floor, would it be pulled into the den where it was found? He scratched his head.

"You seen this?" Dennis asked. He came up behind Bonner and startled him.

"What's that?"

"The fuckin' *LA Times?*" he said and showed him the headline.

INVESTIGATORS BAFFLED BY MYSTERIOUS MURDER, Bonner read.

"The paper reported that the scene at the Castlegate Avenue home appeared odd, not as chaotic as detectives expected in a burglary, and that there'd been no evidence the dog had been drugged, and therefore no explanation as to how a burglar could get past an animal so vicious it wouldn't let police into the yard," Dennis said, quoting from the article.

"Sounds like the *Times* got a source inside the department," Bonner said.

"Shit is making us look bad. We gotta close this one out and get this Bradford cat behind bars where he belongs."

"Lots of things aren't adding up for Daryl Bradford and shit just ain't lookin' good for him, but in spite of that, we're still trying to remain open-minded about this," Bonner said to Dennis, and then added, "We don't want to get tunnel vision on this one suspect and miss a boatload of facts. We have a case to investigate, and no one wants to arrest and possibly imprison the wrong person. We have to look at all the possibilities to paint a clear picture of a suspect or suspects."

In spite of everything Bonner had just said, Dennis still asked a dumb question. "So you think Bradford did it, right?"

Bonner shook his head. "What part of not wanting to get tunnel vision on one thing and miss a boatload of facts didn't you understand?"

"My bad," Dennis replied. "I heard reports that other detectives were checking out a report of a man jumping fences on the south side of the street, connecting to Kelly Park, hours before April died."

"Yeah. A neighbor reported the incident, thinking the man she saw could possibly be the murderer. But come to find out he was an electric company meter reader and was jumping fences to save steps. After a few calls, investigators confirmed that the man had remained on schedule throughout the afternoon and was miles away from Castlegate Avenue during the time of the murder."

At twelve twenty-five that afternoon, all of the detectives involved in the case got together at the precinct to review what they had. Detectives McCaney, Prator, Stinson, Dennis, and Bonner agreed to complete the task of measuring the distance from Daryl's parents' house to the house on Castlegate Avenue. The drive took sixteen minutes. In his statement Daryl said that April had called him at three-thirty, saying she was on her way home. They had obtained cell phone records for both Daryl and April Bradford and were able to confirm that the call had actually come in at three thirty-two. It seemed probable that April had arrived home, as Daryl said in his statements, around three forty-five. Prator recorded the information, making a note to add it to the timeline of events.

# Chapter 21

## *The Coworker Interviews*

Prator and McCaney drove to the post office where Daryl worked and met with his supervisor, William. He had arranged for them to use an office to interview Daryl's coworkers. Many of them had worked with him for several years and could describe his work ethic and character. William was interviewed first, and it didn't take the detectives long to figure out that he and Daryl were friends and that he was trying to protect Daryl. With that knowledge in mind, the detectives made the decision not to push William too hard, but agreed that they would indeed tighten the rope if they didn't get useful information from Daryl's coworkers.

At first, many of the coworkers reported to talk to the detectives, but very few offered anything of help, despite all of them recently expressing their ill feelings and convictions toward Daryl. It was as if they'd held a meeting and were expecting the police to interview them. In each interview, they were all on the same page and insisted they had never heard Daryl talk negatively about April at any time. However, a few of them did mention that they were aware of his relationship with their coworker, Anna Sims.

There were some who defended Daryl, calling him "A good guy. A veteran who loved and fought for his country."

When the detectives left the post office they had nothing more than what they came with. Nothing. They had no concrete evidence or the murder weapon, as the DA told them she needed to initiate an arrest, and they decided not to waste time interviewing Daryl's supervisor again.

"If it comes to it," Prator said to McCaney, "he'll be subpoenaed and have to tell the truth."

"Damn right. He's hidin' somethin', fo' sho," McCaney agreed. "I know his kind."

"It'll be wise for us to find out a little more about Anna Sims," Prator suggested.

"I was thinkin' the same thing," McCaney said. "She might be the key to this whole shit, one way or another!"

Meanwhile that afternoon, Detective Stinson went to the Human Resources building where April worked to interview her coworkers, and discovered very little. Each coworker offered similar indefinite statements.

"She didn't talk much, and when she did," Kendra Rawls, April's supervisor, offered, "she never discussed her personal life, at least not to me."

"Was there anybody that she did speak to?" Detective Stinson asked.

"She'd talk to Elaine Godwin and Anna Sims sometimes, but only talked to me about work issues or concerns."

"Can you give me a sense of her attitude before it happened?" Stinson asked.

"To tell you the truth, I sensed that something was troubling her, but I didn't pry. My only concern was that she did her work efficiently. But I did tell her once that, if she needed someone to talk to, I was here for her. She never came to me so, like I said, I never poked my nose in her business," Kendra explained.

"Is there anything you can tell me from your personal observations?"

"Yes," Kendra began. "Some things were very clear to me. I can't say for sure, of course, that, um . . ." She paused.

"What can't you say for sure?"

"That he was beating her. I honestly believe her husband was beating her."

"What made you believe that?"

"The times she came to work wearing dark sunglasses. Gossip began to stir about her husband beating her and one topic of gossip led to another and another. The work environment became a April soap opera. I had to put a halt to that real quick, due to the amount of errors the employees began making."

"Thank you, Ms. Rawls. You've been very helpful," Stinson said.

"There's something else, too; thinking back to when April first found out she was pregnant, I detected a high level of aggravation about her. I don't know; maybe it was something concerning her pregnancy, but like I said, I didn't pry and had already offered to lend her my ear if she needed it."

"As I said, Ms. Rawls, you've been a big help." Stinson made some notes. "Now, would you mind showing in the first employee please?"

Some coworkers asked about rumors of Daryl's involvement in the murder, but in order to keep things moving, Stinson diverted the conversation by telling them Daryl Bradford had been ruled out as a suspect in the case.

"We're looking at other possibilities, including a burglary," he said.

Stinson noticed that many of the men appeared to be shocked about April's death, while the women cried and grieved.

"Me and April were in the break room eating lunch, and talkin' on the day she died," Adel Fuller said to the detectives. "I noticed how eager she was to leave that day. But because she was so secretive and never hardly talked to anybody, I didn't think much of it. But as far as her work ethic is concerned, she was well-organized, resourceful, professional, and capable of doing her job at a high level. The only thing I found unusual about April was that, unlike the other women who work here, she kept to herself and didn't talk much about her husband or her personal life." Adel suddenly saw an employee who lived near April. "Why don't you talk to Elaine Goodwin," Adel suggested, pointing at Elaine. "I'm sure she could tell you a lot more than I could. They lived not too far from one another and sometimes carpooled. Oh, and Barbara Sims went to school with April and they talked pretty often. There she is sitting at that desk over there, with the long braids and big earrings."

Elaine Goodwin lived on Thorson Street, two blocks from April and Daryl's Castlegate home. Elaine appeared eager to share her firsthand knowledge, perspective, and insight concerning April and Daryl's marriage. She assured Detective Stinson that their marriage was far from the happily-ever-after stuff of fairy tales.

"She knew he was messin' around on her," Elaine said. "But the straw that broke the camel's back was when he gave her STDs twice. Haven't you guys found out about it during this investigation?"

"I'm sure that we have, Ms. Goodwin," Stinson answered.

"That dirty, low-down dog gave her syphilis two different times! Humph; the devil you know, huh?" She raised her eyebrows and turned her head before continuing. "But don't think April was a saint because she wasn't. She was secretive and didn't put her business out there like that, but she confided in me. Until now, I haven't said nothin' to nobody but you about this; but April told me that she was fallin' in love with one of Daryl's friends who'd moved in with them named Tyrone. She called him her new love."

"Really," Stinson said, unable to hide his surprise at that statement. Stinson immediately phoned Prator to tell him there was another person who lived at the crime scene.

"And guess what else; she wasn't pregnant by Daryl. She was carrying Tyrone's baby."

"Tyrone who? You know what his last name is or where I can find him?"

"Tyrone Whitsey. I don't know where you could find him. Like I said, he was living with them."

"So this Tyrone was the father, huh?"

"Yep, that's what she told me. Her new love. But what got me was that he don't have a job. In fact, he's never had a job. From what I gathered, he was one-a those broke men who had never moved outta his mama's house, but knew how to sexually please women. Excuse my French, but to make it plain, a big-dick man who can eat the hell out of some—"

"I get it," Stinson said, cutting her off before she could finish. "I've heard Mrs. Bradford generally kept her business to herself, but she told you all this?"

"She opened up and talked to me sometimes, but I swear, I wish she'da never told me about that. She had already told me Daryl couldn't have babies, so it didn't take a rocket scientist to connect the dots."

"So there was no way her husband could be the father of her child?" Stinson asked, thinking that he had found a motive for the crime. Daryl Bradford found out that his wife was pregnant with another man's baby, lost it, and killed her.

"Anyhow, they started gettin' too open and bold with it, you know. I mean, I saw 'em at Walmart a few times, at Blockbuster renting movies, at the Carson and Cerritos malls. I saw her and Tyrone at Pizza Hut and McDonald's; like I said, it didn't take a rocket scientist to connect the dots. But what really got me was that everybody noticed it but her husband."

"Maybe he did notice," Stinson thoughtfully replied.

Elaine sensed where he was going with this. "You thinking the same thing I am," she said. "Daryl killed her. Who else woulda killed her? The nigga got mad because she fucked his friend and got pregnant by him, that's what I think."

With that information, Stinson continued interviewing coworkers and they begin sharing their knowledge and perceptions with doses of hearsay and honesty.

"Sorry for not being truthful when you first asked me about it," Precious Barnum, a coworker, said. "But I felt bad tellin' you bad things about someone else's marriage when mines is about to fall off a cliff. I heard he knocked out her front tooth, once, and out of guilt, took her to the dentist and had it capped. Other than the other gossip that's floating around here, that's all I have to offer. Talk with Barbara Sims. I'm sure she can offer you more useful information."

Barbara Sims shared what she knew not only about the failed marriage, but also about Daryl's disloyal activities. "She told me she was gonna divorce him," Barbara told Stinson, "but had to wait for the right time to do it. What she meant by 'the right time' I don't know and she never told me. But one thing I do know is that he left her home on Christmas and stayed gone 'til the day after New Year's. Dirty bastard! I hate that man! Lord forgive me for disliking someone to the point that

I hate them, but I hate Daryl Asshole Bradford with a deep-seated passion!"

"How long had she and Tyrone been messing around?"

"After New Year's. That's when she started messin' around with Tyrone. She told me Tyrone's mama had kicked him out and Daryl let him move in with them. That was a big mistake in my opinion, but then again I can't say it was a mistake. I believe that things happen for a reason. Even though Tyrone didn't have a job and wasn't lookin' for one, she told me the reason she liked him so much was because he listened to her, respected her, he was humorous and fun, and what really attracted her was that he made her feel whole, sexually. She also told me he was dark and tall and had a . . ." She caught herself. "Excuse me, Detective. I got a little carried away. You see, Detective, some men forget that just because they don't want you, or they're not attracted to you anymore, that doesn't mean other men aren't. One man's trash is another man's treasure, that's what I always heard. I had an asshole, cheatin', lyin' piece of a husband before, but as soon as I found out about his slick snake ass, I dropped him like a hot potato! Folks gotta be mindful that what goes around comes around twice as hard."

Stinson wholeheartedly agreed with Barbara. *Tyrone could be the key to solving this murder,* Stinson thought, confident that he had uncovered the motive for the murder.

Before Stinson left, he confiscated the hard drive from April's computer. The department's computer experts would inspect it in hopes that it might lead to the sources or possibly a suspect.

Back at the station, Detective Stinson briefed his fellow detectives on his findings, and then wrote his report. McCaney wanted to rush out and arrest Daryl Bradford.

"I been saying from the jump that that son of a bitch was guilty. I'm going to the DA and gettin' a fuckin' warrant and slam-dunk his ass."

"No," Prator said. "We need to talk to Tyrone Whitsey. Maybe he can shed some light on things."

McCaney frowned. "No? What the fuck you mean no? And who the hell is Tyrone?"

"I mean no. I don't think we're there yet. Stinson discovered, after interviewing Elaine, that a man name Tyrone Whitsey lived with the Bradfords."

"Why didn't no one tell me about Tyrone Whitsey?"

Prator rested a hand on McCaney's shoulder, and said, "We just did."

McCaney angrily nodded his head.

"I agree with Prator," Stinson said. "I think we need to find Tyrone Whitsey and get him in the box. For all we know, hell, he may have killed her."

"Look, Mac, I know how bad you want this guy," Prator said, and put his arm around McCaney, "but let's get our ducks in a row first. Which means we continue with the investigation."

"Right," Stinson said.

"We nail down the timeline. Confirm Daryl Bradford's alibi and finish interviewing."

"I know this punk did it. I feel it in my gut," McCaney said. "I want him, and I want him bad! That mutha-fucka shot his pregnant wife three times in the head and killed her." He punched his open hand. "I want that muthafucka."

"He just might be guilty, but let's be sure. And besides, DA Johnson said bring her the murder weapon and we don't have it. So we need to bring her an air-tight case. If you want to call her and brief on what we got," Prator said, and picked up the phone, "go ahead and call her right now. And if she says we got enough for a warrant, then fine."

"But she won't, Mac, 'cause, like Prator said, we ain't there yet," Stinson said.

McCaney took the phone and called DA Johnson. Prator pressed the button to put the call on speaker. After McCaney explained what they had, the DA agreed with Prator.

"Put a .44 Magnum in Daryl Bradford's hand, talk to Tyrone Whitsey to see what he knows. If I feel we've got enough evidence to nail maybe one of them, I'll go to the judge and get a warrant," she said.

When Prator finished with the other detectives, he took out a pen and paper and drew a timeline, recording what he had learned about where April and Daryl Bradford were at what time on that final day. He now knew from April's coworkers that April left work sometime around three-twenty that afternoon. The 911 call came in at seven-thirty. The question all the investigators had to answer was what happened during those four hours and ten minutes?

# Chapter 22

## *Chris and the Time Stamp*

Detectives Prator and McCaney went to interview Daryl's friend, Chris Jenkins. Tension was building in the Jenkins home. While Regina, Chris's wife, thought Daryl was guilty, Chris could not come to grips with even the possibility that his friend could kill his wife.

"You've known Daryl Bradford for a long time," Prator began.

"We go a long way back," Chris said.

After they talked through their history, McCaney started asking more detailed questions.

"What time did Bradford get to your house that day?" McCaney asked.

"About four, four-thirty, maybe," Chris answered.

"And what did you gentlemen do while he was there?"

"We shot some pool and then we watched the Lakers game."

"What time did he leave?" McCaney asked.

"I don't know exactly what time it was, but I'd say about, um, about a quarter to five, somewhere around that time."

"Did he say where he was going once he left there?" Prator asked.

"He said he was going home to April. He said something about April stopping by his parents' house that afternoon to pick up some of his mom's homemade enchilada casserole."

"What about that vicious animal of theirs?" Mc-Caney laughed a little.

"I wouldn't describe Bruno as a vicious animal," Chris replied.

"You wouldn't?" Prator said, raising an eyebrow. "Officers on the scene said they thought they were gonna have to put him down so they could get to the crime scene."

"I don't know about all that. What I can tell you is that I never had a problem with Bruno and been over there at times when children from the neighborhood rode on his back."

"Okay, then what can you tell me about Daryl and April's relationship?" Prator asked.

"Daryl loved April," Chris said. He was not ready to admit any doubts to himself, concerning Daryl.

Prator and McCaney were both mindful of what Johnson had told them: that in order to get a warrant they needed to put a .44 Magnum in Daryl's hand, and talk with Tyrone Whitsey to see what he knew.

With that in mind, Prator pressed forward. "I know from speaking with the family that the Bradford men are all gun enthusiasts. Have you ever seen Daryl Bradford with a .44 Magnum?"

Chris was deep in thought for a few moments and the detectives carefully observed him.

*I can't lie to the police,* Chris thought. *If I don't tell the truth I'll only jeopardize my family and I can't do that! I'm not going to jail for lyin' to the police and I refuse to lie in a courtroom under oath. My statements have to be consistent. One lie will lead to another. I wonder if Daryl came to shoot pool and watch the Lakers game with me that day to build an alibi. I hope like hell you didn't kill April, man, but anyhow, whether you did or not, I don't mean you any harm but I gotta tell the truth.*

Chris released a deep sigh and finally replied, "Yeah, I've seen him with a .44 Magnum about three years ago. I think his father bought it for him."

The detective's hopes were raised, but declined quickly as Chris began to waver.

"I ... I ... I think it was a .44, but I'm not sure. It may have been a .38 or a .357 Magnum or a .45 automatic. I'm not really sure what it was. I ain't into guns. Listen, my mind is so screwed up behind the past events, I don't know if I'll ever recover. I'm sorry."

"That's okay," Prator said to him. "Just take a moment to think. What type of gun was it?"

"To be honest, I just don't remember what kinda gun it was. Like I said, I ain't into guns."

# Chapter 23

## *Meanwhile . . .*

At his office in the police department, Dennis processed evidence, sending it to labs for analysis. They had come away with less than hoped for at the Castlegate Avenue house. It was even more disappointing that he and Bonner never discovered the murder weapon.

That afternoon, detectives went to the Home Depot and to Jack Rabbit Liquor & Jr Market, located on Alondra and Long Beach Boulevard, and to Kelly Park, places that Daryl Bradford professed to have gone. At both stores they presented subpoenas for surveillance tapes from the day of April's murder, and during the time period Daryl said he was in the stores. Both stores had multiple cameras placed at entrances and exits.

With the manager at Jack Rabbit Liquor & Jr Market, Prator loaded the video from the day of the murder into a viewer. First they determined that the time stamp on the video was off by sixty minutes. Possibly, the discrepancy could have been caused by not setting back the timer when daylight saving time ended the previous fall.

The tapes from both stores were collected and brought back to headquarters for further viewing.

# Chapter 24

## *The Mitchell Family*

Detective Stinson met Denise Thomas, known as Necie, at Stanley's sister Lisa's house. As the detective listened, Denise told them a different story from the one Stanley and Kathy had told him. Her account of the time she had spent with April and Daryl over the holidays did not make them sound like a happily married couple. She spoke on Daryl's frequent staying out for two, three nights at a time, and she also spoke on her sister's unhappiness, triggered by emotional, physical, and verbal abuse, as well as the troubles during the marriage.

"That bastard even had the nerve to leave her home alone on Christmas Day!" she said. "That punk turned off his damn cell phone so she couldn't call him! I'm not sure if Daryl killed my sister, but one thing I do know is that they weren't gettin' along at all. I don't understand how she stayed in that fucked-up marriage as long as she did, but see, a bitch like me woulda took his ass out a long time ago! Hot grits, hot grease, poison, cut off his dick, whatever, the punk woulda suffered, believe that! I even heard that he makes sex stops while at work, delivering the mail, and I wouldn't put it past his dirty, low-down ass."

"So you know for a fact that Daryl Bradford was unfaithful to his wife."

"He told me he had been cheatin' on my sister and lyin' to her, but I already knew that, and so did she."

Stanley walked in. Detective Stinson sensed he was irate.

"I want the muthafucka hung that killed my baby, but I wanna be sure y'all got the right person! I don't wanna see Daryl convicted without proof that he did it, and if he did, Lord help him, because believe me, I'll find a way to reach out and touch him no matter where he is!"

Detective Stinson listened as Stanley recounted a story that he read that day in one of the local papers, that deputies might have tampered with evidence to make it appear that Daryl was guilty.

"What do you mean?" Stinson asked.

"Paper says your men could've kicked the glass around from the back door to make it look like the door was open when it was really closed."

Stinson snapped. "I can assure you that nothing like that happened, sir," Stinson insisted.

"We believed that Daryl loved our daughter, but now we wonder. Cheating and lying, leaving her home on Christmas, and using drugs? Those aren't elements of love," Stanley said as Kathy came into the room.

"I wanna believe him too," Kathy said. "But now I don't know if I can."

"Why is that, Mrs. Mitchell?"

"Aside from the information I got from Denise, I been reading the newspapers and I saw details about the physical evidence that raised questions about Daryl's story. Something ain't right about all this, now that I'm able to see a clear picture," she said.

"Did she ever mention anything about Tyrone Whitsey to you?"

"Nothing other than he was a friend of Daryl's who Daryl allowed to live there until he found a job and could do for himself."

"Do you know where I can find Tyrone Whitsey?"

"I only actually met him once. He had just recently moved in with them, Detective, so no, I wouldn't know anything about him."

"Mrs. Mitchell, did you know that your daughter was pregnant?"

"Pregnant?"

"No one told you or you haven't seen it in the newspaper?"

"No. She never mentioned that to us." Kathy became silent and thoughtful. "I do remember April telling me that Daryl couldn't have kids but she never told me why." She thought for a while longer before her eyes got big. "If Daryl couldn't . . ." She caught herself and paused, looking bewildered. "Oh, my God!" she said.

"Is something wrong, Mrs. Mitchell?"

"Oh, my God!" she said again. "If Daryl couldn't produce kids, that means that April . . . was sleeping with someone else." The thought of her angelic and dignified daughter cheating was so overwhelming Kathy's knees buckled.

"Is there proof that Daryl couldn't have kids?" Stinson asked.

"Yes. There are hospital records from a couple times he and April visited a doctor, who recommended Daryl take certain medications and follow some additional procedures, but April said that he wouldn't take the medications and refused to follow the doctor's orders." Kathy felt she had to vomit. "You think Daryl found out April was pregnant and killed her."

"We're actively investigating all possibilities, Mrs. Mitchell."

Mr. Mitchell spoke up. "So what you're sayin' is that my baby was messin' around with another man."

Stinson gave Stanley a silent stare, which was not hard to define.

"Wow," Denise said. "Oh, my God."

# Chapter 25

## *Found Tyrone Whitsey*

It didn't take long for the lab to confirm that Daryl was not the biological father of his wife's baby. Once they obtained the hospital records, that confirmed for Detectives Prator and McCaney that there was no way Daryl could have fathered a child. After that, it didn't take long to find Tyrone. Without a job, money, or anywhere else to go, he had gone back to his mother's house. The detectives quickly brought him in for an interview.

Tyrone appeared saddened and embarrassed at the same time. Ignoring the suspect's emotions and grief, as usual, McCaney pressed forward, using intimidating tactics as well as sarcasm.

"You mean to tell me," McCaney said, frowning. "That you knew she was dead and didn't even bother offering your condolences? And not only were you fucking her, but she was carryin' your baby? What part of the game is that?"

"Listen, man. I saw it on da news and my mama read da newspaper to me 'bout it. What was I s'posed ta do? First thang people gon' think is dat I had sumpin to do wit' it and I didn't. I thought about sayin' sumpin, but then I woulda had ta deal wit' Daryl. It was just too much shit happenin', man, way too fast."

"That's a lame-ass excuse, Mr. Playa Playa," Mc-Caney said. "But what can we expect comin' from somebody like you? Anyway, so, you were fuckin' your friend's wife, just beatin' that pussy up like you owned it, huh?"

"She was my new love," said the baby-faced, dark-complexioned, six foot four, slim, and inarticulate man. He smiled and briefly drifted into la-la land, then continued his response.

"Me and April's relationship didn't start like y'all think it did. That conceited nigga was never there," Tyrone stated, developing a frown.

"So you decided to take his place, huh?" McCaney sarcastically said. "Yeah, you kept his side of the bed warm while he was out, right?"

"Where was he?" Prator asked.

"He was always out chasin' street bitches and gettin' his freak on, as he put it, with his so-called 'prize bitch' Anna Sims or other bitches he fucked."

"And he had no problem leaving you home alone with his wife?" Prator said.

"No, that didn't stop him from goin' out in the streets to do his drugs and fuckin' those street hoes. Sometimes he wouldn't come home for two, three, four days at a time, and when he did come home, guilt tore him up so bad, he came in and start talkin' crazy to April."

"What do you mean, talkin' crazy?" Prator asked.

"You know, accusin' her of fuckin' another man."

"Hell, you was fuckin' her, so she was messin' around," McCaney said.

Tyrone ignored the comment and jumped to another subject. "He was always degradin' me, 'cause I lived with him and didn't have a damn job. I got construction skills like layin' tile, roofin', plumbin', framin' houses and buildings, I got electrical skills; man, I can damn near build a house from da ground up, and—"

McCaney rudely cut him off. "How else you gon' build a got-damn house, from the sky down?" he sarcastically asked. "I hate when people say, 'my house was built from the ground up' or 'I know somebody who had their house built from the ground up.' That some stupid-ass shit! Like the muthafucka can be built from the sky down." He released a deep sigh.

Prator continued, "You got construction skills, but you're just lazy, right?"

"Whatever," Tyrone replied and continued. "I had a job one time workin' for Cleveland Thomas, who owned Thomas Construction Company. He fired me, though, 'cause I was late to work every day my first week. Jus' wasn't used to gettin' up dat time of mornin', you feel me? Anyway, Daryl thought he was Mr. Big Stuff ever since we was kids. He was kinda cool back in da days; you know what I'm sayin'? He used to let me wear some of his clothes to school. He let me wear his Tims a few times. He shared his lunch wit' me, but I really think he did that was so he could talk about me afterward 'cause we was poor. My mama cleaned people's houses for a livin' and he was born wit' a silver spoon in his mouth. Him and his brothers—as a matter of fact, his whole damn family—thought they was betta than me and a whole lotta other people, 'cause they got that high-yellow complexion and a little money, and we dark black and was poor."

"Is that a fact?" McCaney said, shaking his head. "Ain't too much changed since then, huh?"

Tyrone did not read between the lines. "You know how some of those light-skinned people think they ain't got black in 'em and think they betta than dark people?"

Both Prator and McCaney were tired of Tyrone's bullshit talk and wanted facts and evidence.

"Let's get back to you and April Bradford," Prator recommended.

"My new love," Tyrone said, smiling. "Like I said, April was tired of Daryl's shit, know what I'm sayin'? She needed somebody to talk to and somebody to listen to her, you feel me? She said it best when she said 'shit happens when vows are broke.'"

"I feel you, all right," McCaney said and rolled his eyes. "The word is 'broken,' not 'broke.'"

"Whateva, you know what I mean. Anyway, she needed a strong shoulder to lean on," Tyrone continued. "You feel me? She was a good woman, man, and I can say dat. Dat low-down punk didn't deserve her! As far as I'm concerned, she mighta been his wife, but she was and will always be my woman. My new love. She said I was her bridge over troubled waters." He drifted into la-la land, smiling.

Prator stayed on point. "Snap out of it, Tyrone," Prator said, snapping his finger. "So you did know she was pregnant and carrying your child?"

"Yeah, she told me," Tyrone said with pride. "And as far as my son goes, I'm gon' be honest wit' y'all, I wanted to take dat muthafucka out for what he did, but dat wouldn'ta bought April back. Dat was my flesh and blood, my only child, you feel me, and for dat nigga to jus' . . . jus' . . . ." Tyrone became emotional and cried. "Jus' kill what was mines, I . . . I . . . I wanted to take him out. But I decided not to, 'cause da nigga wasn't worth me doin' da rest of my life in prison, so I left it alone. I damn sho ain't gon' put myself in a position to let da white man or no man tell me when I can eat, sleep, and take a got-damn shower, you feel me? And I ain't into eatin' TV dinners. I like soul food, barbeque, catfish, neck bones, candied yams, and steaks and shit. One of my homies told me dat ain't even no mirrors in jail; dat you can't even look at yo'self. I need to look at myself at least four, five times a day, you feel me? April used to call me baby face and I used to call her my queen."

Prator and McCaney exchanged looks, nodding in disgust, as if they were thinking the same exact thing: *Either this guy is a damn good actor, or he's telling the truth.*

"So you had no problem with the baby being yours?" Prator asked.

"No. I was the happiest man in da world. I was gonna be a daddy."

"Were you still living with the Bradfords the day of the murder?" Prator asked.

"Yeah, I was still livin' there."

"And it didn't bother you that you were fucking your so-called friend's wife and living free in his house? And don't give me no long-ass answer. Just answer the gotdamn question," McCaney said.

"He wasn't never there, and like I said, when he did come home he was da biggest asshole you'd ever wanna meet. I swear he was! He always called her bitch and ho and whatever other degradin' name dat came to his mind. I'm tellin' y'all, he don' said some shit to me dat made me wanna kill 'em right on da spot, but—"

McCaney rudely cut him off. "Tell us about that, Davis."

"A'right. One night he came in pissed off, after not comin' home for three days. Me and April knew he was out cheatin', but we didn't talk about it, you feel me; we talked about us. Dat's what gave us hope. We never did really talk about him or what he did, it wasn't no use to. We talked about us, you feel me?"

An agitated McCaney nodded in a disgusting manner, about to blow a fuse. "Go on, Mr. Davis. Continue, but continue with substance, not bullshit."

"Anyway, he walked in talkin' shit as usual, accusin' April of fuckin' another man, when I was the one really hittin' it. Man, I came up out my room and took up for her like I always do, and like he always did, he started on me."

"What did he say to you?" McCaney asked.

"He was sayin' some shit like, 'You ain't shit, never have been shit, and never will be shit, thanks to yo' slut mama!'"

"How'd that make you feel?" Prator asked.

"It made me feel bad, him talkin' about my mama."

"What else did he say?"

"He straight out said, 'That bitch got eight kids, all by different niggas, and that's why you so fucked up in the head, unstable, pathetic, and ain't neva' tried to do a damn thing with your life!'"

"What did you say to him?"

"That I wasn't unstable and pathetic," Tyrone insisted.

"Okay."

"'It's true,' he said, 'yeah, blame yo' slut mama! I bet you don't even know who your real daddy is, do you? I bet yo' mama had you callin' other niggas Daddy, didn't she?'"

The detectives noticed rage building in Tyrone, but allowed him to continue without interrupting him.

"I snapped, and lost it when he started talkin' shit about my mama!" Tyrone explained. "You can talk about me all you want, but don't say nothin' outta line 'bout my mama!"

Prator and McCaney looked at one another.

"Go on, Mr. Davis," Prator said. His years of experience told him that guys like Tyrone were more likely to sit quietly and take it, than to get up and do something about it.

"Anyway," Tyrone continued, "I charged at dat punk, swinging, saying, 'That's why I fu . . .' But I caught myself."

"How did Bradford react?"

"He hit me hard in the stomach and took my wind, dat's how he reacted. I gasped to breathe, but da only thing I could do was stand there and hold my stomach. I was paralyzed. Then he was yellin' shit like, 'That's why you failed?' He thought I was about to say 'fail' when I was really about to say, 'That's why I fucked your wife!' Anyway, he stood over me and kept yellin', 'Is that what you were gonna say? You confessin' dat yo' mama is da reason dat you failed in life, aren't you? Tell me somethin' man; what did you expect out of life, givin' up and doin' nuttin', huh? Tell me, what did you expect by doin' nothin'? Nothin' from nothin' leaves nothin', ol' stupid, illiterate muthafucka! Like I said, blame yo' got-damn mama,'" Tyrone told the detectives.

"What did you say to that, Mr. Davis?" Prator asked, trying hard to hold back his laughter.

"All I could do was hold my stomach and listen to his shit. Anyway, he kept talkin' shit."

"What was he sayin' then?" McCaney asked.

"'I'm ex-military, bitch, you musta forgot! Nigga, I can take you out jus' like dat!'" Tyrone snapped his fingers, emphasizing his point. "'And if you eva' try dat shit again, I will take you da fuck out! It ain't my fault you can't handle the truth about yo' mama's slut history.'"

"What happened after that?"

"He had his way wit' me and kicked my ass, yeah, he did dat. I was out of it a few minutes and when I came to, he was screamin' again, sayin', 'I'm God up in dis muthafucka, y'all bitches better recognize! Yeah, I'm da hog wit' da big balls! I'm the nigga who walk light, but carry a big stick! Y'all betta start respectin' me, or else! I just thought of somethin'. You know what; both of y'all sorry muthafuckas deserve each other. 'Cause neither one-a y'all ain't shit! Don't nobody want you, April, you ain't nuttin' but used and damaged goods; and, Tyrone, nobody damn sho want your broke, no-job ass! Both of y'all are way beneath me, way beneath me, so da next time you think about comin' weak at a strong nigga like me, do yourself a favor and dismiss dat thought!'" Tyrone claimed to still remember Daryl's words clearly, as if he'd said them. Then he told the detectives about another episode.

"One time he came home 'bout four in da mornin', drunk and high off dat shit, and snatched April outta bed and started cussin' her out, accusin' her of fuckin' somebody else."

"What you're tellin' me is that he'd be out all night and then he'd come home and accuse her of fucking somebody else?" McCaney said.

"Which she was. She was fucking you, Mr. Davis. Do you think he knew what the two of you were up to?" Prator asked.

"Nah. I don't think he knew. My guess is dat guilt was tearin' him up again, you know. Me and her had been together all dat day and night, so he was just trippin' again."

"That's my point, Mr. Davis," Prator said. "The two of you had been together all day; maybe he saw you."

"Da only time we left da house was to go to Blockbuster."

"Y'all didn't go to McDonald's?" McCaney asked. He had read Stinson's report on his interview with Elaine Goodwin and remembered reading that they been seen out together quite often. Daryl having seen them together would strengthen his motive for murdering his wife. McCaney was still determined to prove that Daryl Bradford had killed her.

"Not dat night. Anyway, I heard him yellin' and I could hear her screamin' and cryin'. I heard shit fallin' everywhere, heard her bein' slammed against da wall and slapped, so I jumped outta bed and went up in there, hopin' he would stop, but again, he started on me."

"What he say to you this time, Mr. Davis?" Prator asked.

"'Stay da fuck outta my business or get da hell outta my house! Jobless, hopeless, pitiful piece of shit! You gotta bunch of damn nerve, you broke, food-stamp-card-carrying, sorry muthafucka! Get da fuck outta here before I beat yo' ass again and put you outta my house! You stupid as da day is long, nigga! You gotta be a damn fool to bite da hand dat feed you!' Dat's da kinda shit he was sayin'."

"And that's why she turned to you?" Prator asked sarcastically, but Tyrone didn't pick up on it.

"It didn't start out dat way. And I never planned for it to happen. At first I was a shoulder for her to lean on, you feel me? I listened to her problems and concerns, we laughed together, watched movies together, and we danced to oldies, played cards and dominoes. Then one day, out of da blue, while lookin' at each other, we kissed, and, man, I'm tellin' y'all, dat was da kiss of life. She held me and kissed me like she'd been waitin' for me all her life. Dat's when I knew we loved each other." He smiled, while reminiscing, staring off into space.

"So much for the love shit; on with the story, Davis," McCaney rudely said.

"Anyway," Tyrone continued, "one thing led to another and da next thing you know, we was makin' love, as she put it, every day, as much as we could do it. I called it fuckin', but she didn't like dat word, she called it 'makin' love.' I was really feelin' her, man, and trust me, she was feelin' me too." Tyrone suddenly drifted off into la-la land again, smiling. "Sometimes, outta hate for Daryl, I tried killin' da pussy, to get back at him, knowin' she liked it gentle, slow, and deep, you feel me? I knew I was hurtin' her. God really looked out for me down there, you know what I mean? Da louder she yelled from da dick, da harder and rougher I drilled her, tryin' to kill da pussy, but da last thing I wanted to do was hurt her. He was da one I hated, not her, but I jus' lost it for a few moments, you know what I'm sayin'?"

The detectives glared at one another, and continued listening to the long-winded suspect, and Prator tried to keep in mind that he was as much a suspect in this case as Daryl Bradford and Anna Sims. Despite what he was saying, Tyrone could have just as easily killed April Bradford, but Prator understood that only time and the evidence would tell.

As for McCaney, he still believed that Daryl Bradford was guilty and that they were just wasting their time with Tyrone Whitsey.

"We fell in love wit' each other just like dat." He snapped his fingers again, stressing his point. "It was all good, and I mean all good. It was his loss and our gain, dat's da way we saw it. Every time he came home talkin' shit, he'd leave afterward and me and her would do our thang. Dat's how much attention he paid to her. As fine and intelligent as she was, can you believe he chose to fuck street bitches over her? He didn't deserve April, I'm tellin' y'all; he didn't deserve her."

Prator jumped in. "So you deserved her, right?"

Before Tyrone could answer the question, McCaney put his two cents in. "Sounds like you and April were made for each other, huh? A love story made on earth, to be continued in heaven, right?"

"Yep. My new love. You damn right we gon' hook back up in heaven if da good Lord make it happen. It was what it was. And to answer your question, Detective Prator, yeah, I deserved her. Nah, put it like dis: we deserved and wanted each other, dat's da way I see it."

McCaney laughed out loud. "Without a job, how was your broke ass gonna take care of her and a baby?"

The degrading question didn't seem to bother Tyrone at all. "We talked about dat damn near every day, before and after we fuc . . . . Oops, my bad. I mean before and after we made love. She was gon' pay for me to go to truck driving school. She said da school was three months, and it cost twenty-five hundred dollars. She said she knew three people who had jus' graduated from da school and was already working, makin' fourteen to eighteen dollars an hour and at home every night. She said she didn't want me to go over the road 'cause I'd only be home once a week, and sometimes I might not come home for a month or two. But yeah, we had talked about dat. I was ready to do da right thang for da sake of her and my son."

"Sounds like you had it made, Davis. A man with a plan, huh?" Prator sarcastically said.

"Yeah, dat's what I thought too, but dat fuckin' Daryl." He frowned, clinching his fist. "I swear I wanna do dat nigga, man! Listen, I loved April and I swear to y'all I ain't had nothin' to do wit' killin' her! She meant more to me alive than dead, and dat's real talk. Dat baby woulda been my first child."

He stood and became emotional. "Daryl should be da one dead, not April! I hate dat muthafucka! Ever since dat fool got outta da military he thought he was better than me and everybody else! I kept tellin' him he changed, but he couldn't see it! And you know what really pissed me off: when he talked to other bitches on the phone in April's face, like she didn't even exist or wasn't in da room! I hate dat muthafucka! You know he even told me he fucked Anna, his prize bitch, in his and April's bed! How low can you go, man! How low can you go?

"Listen; I know I was wrong for what I did by fuckin' my friend's wife, but I can't take dat back. I tried talkin' her outta tellin' him she was pregnant, but she said she wanted him to know da truth. She said she didn't wanna live a lie. I felt bad and was confused and didn't know what to do or how I was gonna face Daryl if she told him, so I split and went to mama for help. Dat's why I had ta get outta dodge. But he killed her, I know he did! He killed her when she told him about me and her; dat's how it went down, I bet it did! He probably wanted to kill me, too, but I was outta there. Look; like I said, I fucked up by fuckin' my friend's wife, but I still don't regret it today. She was my girl and I loved her and she loved me. Nobody in dis world would ever do nothin' foul to her, but Daryl!"

McCaney interrupted. "So you won't have a problem testifying to your relationship with her and your participation in court, right?"

"Hell no, I won't! Fuck Daryl!" he angrily yelled. "Dat muthafucka killed my woman and my baby. His punk ass deserves to rot in prison, then rot in hell! I can't wait to testify, fuck him! Like I said before; she mighta been his wife, but she was my woman, and since she can't speak up for herself, I'm gon' do it for her!"

*There it is,* thought the detectives, *a strong motive for Daryl Bradford to murder his wife.* They still needed the gun, but Tyrone gave him a reason for the gun to be in his hand.

"Have you ever saw Daryl with a .44 Magnum?"

"I ain't neva' seen him wit' a .44," Tyrone answered. "But I seen him wit' a .22 and I think it was a .38 Special he showed me, too. I ain't gon' sit here and lie and say I saw him with somethin' I didn't. April and my mama always said dat one lie leads to another, and another."

Tyrone was then dismissed, but instructed not to leave town until the dust completely settled and the case was closed.

# Chapter 26

## *Bring Him In*

As soon as Tyrone left, McCaney was on the phone with the DA. And once again, Prator put the call on speaker. McCaney advised her that he and his partner had just completed the interview of Tyrone Whitsey and that he felt strongly that they had enough for an arrest warrant for Daryl Bradford, for the murder of his wife.

"Look, Detective," DA Johnson said. "I respect the fact that your gut tells you that Bradford is our man; however, I still think you need to find the murder weapon and put it in his hands. That will be the only way I see to put the icing on the cake."

McCaney did not plan to take no for an answer; at least, not right off without expressing his view and beliefs. "I think with the testimony of Tyrone Whitsey that gives Bradford the motive to kill his wife. I mean it practically puts the gun in his hand," McCaney all but pleaded.

It was obvious to Johnson that the detective wanted this guy badly. "Okay, Detective, you can bring him in, but don't arrest him. Just bring him in for question- ing."

McCaney's adrenalin was flowing rapidly. "Once I get his ass in the box and sweat him, this punk will talk. I've seen his kind a million times. He'll talk all right," McCaney said quickly, and hung up the phone while he was still ahead and had not heard any of Johnson's exceptions.

"Where you going?" Prator asked.

"Where do you think? I'm going to slam-dunk a cold-blooded killer, that's where I'm goin'."

"No," Prator insisted.

"No. What the fuck you mean no? The DA just told me I could get him in the box."

"I know, but send a unit to pick him up and bring him in. If you go it will escalate to something else and I don't need that shit," Prator said. "You need to pull back on your emotions on this one, Mac; you're too intense. I don't want any mistakes."

Reluctantly, McCaney agreed and an hour later they had Daryl in the interrogation room. Prator did not waste any time drilling Daryl.

"Why didn't you tell us about Tyrone Whitsey?"

"Why; should I have?" Daryl replied, shocked by the question. "He's not relevant in this."

McCaney furiously got in Daryl's face. "The hell he's not relevant!" McCaney yelled, standing over Daryl. "He's the father of your wife's baby! I told you from the get-go, I felt you were hidin' somethin', and here it is!"

Daryl snapped and stood up. "Fuck you, man! I ain't hidin' a damn thing!"

They stood face to face, like two mad pit bulls.

"Sit your ass down before I knock you down, fool!"

Prator jumped up quickly and separated Daryl and McCaney. Daryl sat down and Prator pulled his partner off to the side.

"Why don't you sit this one out, Mac? You're too close. Like I said, you need to pull back a little."

"Okay, but I'm not leaving. I'll just sit over there."

At that point, Prator took over the questioning, allowing his partner to cool off. "I'm gonna tell you what we already know," Prator calmly said. "And then I'll tell you what I think!"

"Am I under arrest?" Daryl asked.

"No, we just have some questions we'd like to ask you about Tyrone Whitsey."

"What do you think you already know?"

"We know for a fact that Tyrone Whitsey, your friend who you let move into your home, was bangin' your wife, and we know through DNA that the baby wasn't yours."

McCaney jumped up, wanting to deliver the next bombshell. "And we know that you're impotent and carry weak-ass sperm! How 'bout that, Prator: an alleged strong, cocky, military man with weak, ineffective sperm?" McCaney chuckled, trying to get next to Daryl.

Prator looked disapprovingly at his partner and then resumed the interview. "My theory now, Mr. Bradford, is that your wife told you that she was fuckin' Tyrone and was pregnant by him, and, not being able to handle the truth, you killed her in cold blood!"

McCaney jumped in again. "That's exactly what happened! Now tell me why the hell would you say Tyrone isn't relevant?"

"Fuck both of y'all and y'all theories, too!" Daryl yelled, jumping from his chair. "Y'all don't know what you talkin' about!"

"You couldn't handle the truth, huh, Bradford? That was a pretty big pill to swallow, wasn't it? Hell, I probably couldn't have taken it either. Your best friend fuckin' your wife after you allowed him to move in your crib? Damn, that's some shit, man. Imagine that. But I'll tell you what, Bradford; make it easy on yourself and save all of us some time; confess and tell us how you did it, and we'll work some—"

Daryl snapped, cut off the detective, and angrily stood up once again. "Fuck you and kiss my yellow ass! I ain't had shit to do with killin' April! And so got-damn what if I knew the baby wasn't mines? That don't prove a goddamn thing! Like I said, kiss my yellow ass!"

McCaney got in Daryl's face again. Prator stood back and allowed his partner to do his thing, uninterrupted.

"I despise muthafuckas like you, Bradford," Mc-Caney said. "You know that? You see, Bradford, I know all about you; yes, I do. I made it my business to do my homework. Oh yeah, I know all about the Oriental bitches you fucked with overseas, and caught that shit from, and then brought it home to your wife. I know that you're an undercover crackhead. Oh yeah, I know all about it. And I know that you're a disease-carryin' muthafucka who thinks his shit don't stink. Oh yeah, I made it my business to do my homework on you, Bradford. So what that means, Bradford, is that every bitch you fucked recently caught that shit from you and gave it to somebody else. Oh yeah. And according to your medical records, you are a carrier. A fuckin' carrier, man! That means that you'll have that shit for the rest of your miserable life. You been spreadin' that shit like peanut butter, homie. A muthafuckin' outbreak, caused by you. Ain't that a bitch! People all over the world are suffering because of you! And you got the nerve to—"

Daryl, not being able to handle the truth, snapped, "You don't know what the fuck you talkin' about!"

"Want me to show you proof? Or would like to hear witnesses testify to what your wife told them? Huh? Speak up, boy."

"Fuck you!"

"No, fuck you! And we'll see who gets fucked. Disease-carryin' muthafucka!"

Meanwhile, Chris Jenkins's wife, Regina, walked into the station and asked to speak to somebody about the Bradford case. Since Prator and McCaney were busy interrogating Daryl, Detective Stinson came out to speak with her. The detective saw the petite and classy African American woman with Chris next to her. While her husband, who steadfastly defended Daryl, waited in a hallway, Regina met privately with Stinson, telling him about the problems in April's marriage, including the times she had witnessed Daryl call his wife demeaning names like bitch, ho, muthafucka, stupid, and dumb. Throughout the interview, Regina was emotional and very upset.

"Their problems spilled over into our marriage," Regina confessed. "And for the sake of our marriage I made the decision not to spend as much time with April as I had been. It was difficult, but I had to do what I had to do to save my own marriage."

"To your knowledge," Stinson asked, "was Daryl physically abusive to her?"

"Yes, he was. She told me about all of the times that he slammed her against the wall when she didn't agree with him or during a heated argument. She also told me about a time that he slapped her for mentioning past-due bills in the presence of company. She told me he had knocked out her tooth once, and took her to have it capped afterward. I don't know how the hell she put up with his shit for all these years. Daryl, I give it to him, is a damn good actor who puts on a front in public, and whenever they were around family or friends it was as if they were that perfect, loving, and inseparable couple. Believe me, Detective, that deceptive piece of shit had a helluva dark side to him."

The detective decided to drop a bomb on Regina to see her reaction, wondering if she was already aware of the situation. "Did you know that April was pregnant?"

"No, I didn't."

"Well, she was. And her unborn child," Stinson said, looking into her eyes, "does not belong to Daryl. Tyrone Whitsey, Daryl's friend who he allowed to move into the home, is the actual father. That has been proven through DNA."

Regina was shocked, as she sat there wide-eyed with an open mouth, as if she had seen a ghost. "No way," she said. "Uh-uh, I don't believe that."

"Whether you believe it or not, Mrs. Jenkins, it's a fact. DNA does not lie."

The news only proved to increase her suspicions toward Daryl. "Well, if that's true, there it is there! His motive to kill April and the baby was because, in his crazy mind, neither April or the baby were his! The way he thinks, he'd figure she wasn't his because she cheated on him. And there was no way on earth he would be a father to a baby that wasn't his. If people found out it was actually his friend's baby that would tarnish his image. Daryl couldn't allow that. The one thing Daryl could not tolerate was embarrassment. Yep, there it is, he killed them. I know he did."

"That's for a court and a jury to decide, Mrs. Jenkins. Thanks for your input and time."

"You're welcome," Regina said and rushed out of the office. She was eager to tell her husband about the baby.

# Chapter 27

## *Canvas the Neighborhood*

The Gathings family was well liked in the neighborhood. They were thought of as good people. They lived with their three young kids directly behind the Bradfords. The uniformed officers who were canvassing the neighborhood, thinking that somebody might have heard something, rang the bell.

After the officers explained what they wanted, the children—Jonasia Gathings, age nine; Antonio Gathings, age seven; and Robert Jr., age six—told the police their story.

They arrived home on the school bus at approximately four o'clock that Monday afternoon. Afterward they did homework, and after that they watched cartoons in the den. Their father had taken a couple of pain pills and had fallen asleep. During the cartoons, they heard a noise.

"What did it sound like?" the officer asked.

"Pow! pow! pow!" Jonasia said.

"I thought it was firecrackers," Antonio said.

"Sounded like a gun, though," Jonasia added.

Robert Jr. nodded, agreeing with his brother. "Yep, it sounded like somebody was shootin' at our house," Robert Jr. said, and like always when he spoke, he began laughing.

Antonio added another assumption. "I thought the coyote was shootin' at Bugs Bunny on TV."

"Couldn't been," Jonasia said quickly. "The coyote didn't have a gun. You talkin' about Yosemite Sam."

The kids laughed simultaneously as the officer began drawing conclusions. If the kids were telling the truth, and heard the shots at the time they said, then Daryl couldn't have murdered April. Bradford would have been en route to or at Jack Rabbit Liquor & Jr Market.

Still, there were questions about the kids' account. It seemed likely that all of them had heard something, but what? Were their memories reliable enough to determine a time?

Another factor that made their account even more questionable was the report of a neighbor who heard and saw a truck backfire around the time the Gathings kids heard the noise. He had even given a description of the truck to police. Instead of a gunshot, could that have been what the kids heard?

Other neighbors who resided on Castlegate Avenue and the surrounding streets wondered about the time of the gunshots too, speculating on why no one else heard anything. Some decided that if the gunshot happened between three fifty-five and four twenty-five, when school buses travel down the street, stopping every few blocks and setting their brakes with a loud noise, no one would have paid attention.

"At that time of day, I would have thought it was just a loud bus," most neighbors said.

The more interesting alternative theory for the officers involved another of the Bradfords' neighbors. The teenager who lived next door to the Bradfords could be angry enough to have resorted to violence. The kid went by the name of Killa Mike.

Michael Thomas, aka Killa Mike, was a dark-complexioned reputed bully, who both sold and smoked marijuana, and ditched school on a regular basis. Neighborhood rumors had it that Michael had been seen, but not caught, breaking in vehicles, stealing stereos, batteries, and other valuables one could easily exchange for quick cash.

The reputable thug was also known to hang out after school and sell joints of marijuana, crack, and ecstasy, while guzzling from a forty-ounce bottle of Olde English 800. What really caught the detectives' attention about Thomas was it had been stated that he had a thing for older women.

Was it possible that Michael Thomas was banging April too? Was it also possible that Michael Thomas discovered that Tyrone was banging April and got angry enough to kill her behind it, maybe obsessed with her?

Another neighbor reported that they had seen April coming from the Thomas house on a few occasions. April told the neighbor that she had gone there a couple of times, once to ask him to turn down that loud rap music. Another time, April had gone there to let his single-parent mother know that she had seen Michael at home during school hours, with a woman she knew for certain was a dopehead, who lived a few blocks away. April had heard the woman's sex cries from an open window, and also reported that to Thomas's mother.

Was that enough for him to kill her?

"April actually liked Michael Thomas," a nosy neighbor said. "She wasn't the type of person who had hate in her heart. She told on him, wanting his mother to know what he was up to while she was out earning a living. She was concerned about his future, seeing that he was headed in the wrong direction."

On the block, Thomas wasn't the most popular teenager. When his mother was out of town with a boyfriend, he had thrown a party, which included practically every thug from nearby neighborhoods, such as The South Side, N-Hood, Atlantic Drive, Kelly Park, Santana Block, Palmer Block, and Spook Town affiliates; that was until gang members from Cedar Block, The Luders Park Mob, Lime Hood, and Fruit Town Piru's shot it up.

The party had prompted numerous complaints, another neighbor said, certain that Thomas had stolen his spoke hubcaps.

"He was still a decent kid," another neighbor said in Thomas's defense. "He looked out for kids and played ball with 'em sometimes; if he wasn't playing with 'em, he'd get balls out of the streets for 'em to prevent them from running in the streets, getting hit by a car. He bought the kids ice cream and sweets from the ice cream truck; as far as I'm concerned, Michael has never been a major problem. There's nothing wrong with a teenage boy ditching school to get a piece of pussy, you know. I'm quite sure you've engaged in such things during your teens, Officer."

Once the uniformed officers discussed their findings with the detectives, McCaney remained convinced that Daryl was undoubtedly April's killer. Prator insisted on following protocol: that they check out all leads.

At that point, even though Daryl was still the Detective's primary suspect, wanting to leave no stones unturned, they decided to check out Michael Thomas. The detectives found out from another neighbor that Thomas sold blunts and crack. They described the teenager as a serious threat to the neighborhood.

What did interest the detectives was that Michael Thomas had lied about his whereabouts during the time of the murder. When questioned by the detectives with his mother beside him, the thug teenager insisted he had been in school on January 11. When the detectives checked his attendance record, they discovered he had not been to school in eight days. Then something else happened to shine a light on Michael Thomas. A report came in from the Compton Police Department about a .44 Magnum found by an elderly man in a canal behind the Wilmington Arms, a ruthless village of low-income apartments. McCaney and Prator rushed to the scene with high hopes.

The weapon was rusty, as if it had been outside in the rain for a long period. It was recovered with a brown jewelry box. On the lid were the initials E.B. Sr.

McCaney never took custody of the box, but he did sign for the gun and had it tested against the shells they found at the Bradford crime scene, hopeful to tie it to the unsolved murder.

The gun, it was soon discovered, was registered to Emerson Bell Sr., and after further investigation, detectives learned that Emerson Bell Sr. had died years earlier and that his son Emerson Bell Jr. was a crack smoker, and also a customer of Michael Thomas's.

"This is interesting," McCaney said.

"You got that shit right," Prator agreed. "Maybe Daryl Bradford ain't our guy after all."

"I know things aren't what they always seem, but, man, my gut tells me that Daryl Bradford is guilty of killing his wife! I sense that he is somehow connected to this shit. I know he is, Prator!"

"Time and evidence will tell," Prator replied.

When interviewed, Emerson Bell Jr. confessed to exchanging the gun for drugs to a teenage drug dealer named Killa Mike. McCaney took the gun into evidence and submitted it to the lab for testing.

The small-time drug dealer had questions to answer: Why did he lie? Where was he the day of the murder? Had he been involved in a sexual affair with April Bradford? Was he somehow involved in April Bradford's murder? Had Daryl Bradford paid him off for the hit, knowing he was a money-hungry and easily manipulated teenager? Had Thomas killed April using Emerson Bell's gun then afterward dumped it in the canal?

Prator sent a unit to pick up Michael Thomas at his residence, directly next door to the Bradford home. The detectives didn't want to question him again in front of his mother, so they thought it best to bring him to the station for questioning. Since he was underage, Prator arranged for a representative from children services to be present.

"You lied to us last time we talked, Michael," Prator began when he entered the interrogation room.

"What I lie about?" Michael asked.

"You lied about where you were at the time of the murder," Prator said calmly. "That wasn't very nice. Lying to a police officer is a serious felony, son. So let's start there, shall we? Where were you yesterday between four and five?"

Michael looked around the room and then at the detective. "I just told you that I was at school 'cause my mama was there."

"Okay," McCaney said. "We get that. Now tell us, where you were yesterday?"

"I did go to school, but I left early, and was just hangin' out."

"Selling drugs?" Prator asked.

"I don't know what you talkin' 'bout, Officer."

"Look, asshole, everybody and his mama knows that you sell crack and weed, and go by the name of Killa

Mike, okay?" McCaney said. "So don't bullshit me, homie."

"This is a homicide investigation, so right now, I couldn't care less about your little piss-ant dope business," Prator said. "Are we clear?"

"Yeah."

"So, Killa Mike, since that's what you like to go by, why don't you walk me through your day from the time you left school," Prator insisted.

"I left school after fourth period, at about two o'clock," Michael began.

"Where did you go?" McCaney asked.

"My homeboy EB picked me up and drove me home."

"What the fuck is an EB?" McCaney asked even though he already knew. "We need you to be clearer about what you say."

"His slave name is Emerson Bell."

"Slave name?" Prator asked.

"Yeah, slave name. I'm practicin' to be a Muslim, and I was told dat we all got slave names, you feel me?"

McCaney shook his head in disgust.

"Go ahead," Prator said. "So tell us, what did you two pillars of society do then?"

"I scooped up my stash—"

"Of crack and marijuana?" McCaney said.

"Whatever you say, Officer. Anyway, we drove around in EB's car smoking blunts."

"Where did you guys go?" Prator asked.

"Just crusin', checkin' out da honeys, feel me? Then we went back to my crib 'bout three-thirty or sumpin like dat."

"What you go back there for?" McCaney asked.

"I was hungry, so we got some grub at Bill's Burgers hamburger stand on White Street and Alondra. While we was eating, we was schemin' on a small-time hustler who lived on da other side of town. He owed me fifty dollars for two months and ac' like he wasn't gon' pay up."

"What did you do?" Prator asked.

"I used my cell to call a nigga named Richard, who drove over and met us ten minutes later. He brought anotha nigga wit' him named Steve."

"What did you call them for?" Prator asked.

"They's my lynch mob," Michael said and laughed a little.

"Whatever," McCaney said, shaking his head.

"What then, Killa?" Prator asked.

"I told EB to roll to da south side. We was gonna either collect or beat down da nigga dat owed me money."

"This guy, Bell, he's twice your age. What's he doin' rollin' around with you minor-league pee-wee thugs?" McCaney asked.

"He got a car and he like to get high for free. He took me to cop and I always break him off a little sumpin-sumpin. Or sometimes he'll just throw me the keys, long as I throw him a little sumpin for his head and flip him some gas money," Michael said, clearly becoming bolder about his involvement in the dope game. "He be ready for whatever."

"Let's talk about you and EB's gun. It's a .44 Mag, ain't it?" Prator asked. By then, the detectives knew that the gun McCaney processed from Bell was not the murder weapon.

"Yep. With big-ass bullets, too."

"So what happened when you rolled to the south side?" Prator asked.

"We rolled up on dis house, on Burris Street. Nu-Nu was standing out front."

"Real name?"

"Walter Newton."

"Did you get your money?" McCaney asked.

Michael paused and looked around the room. He wasn't anxious to tell the rest of the story.

"What happened, Killa Mike?" McCaney pressed.

"That muthafucka beat da shit outta me, man, dat's what happened," Michael finally said and everybody laughed.

"That shit ain't funny, man," Michael sadly said.

"What happened to your so-called lynch mob?"

"They just stood there and watched me get my ass kicked."

"They didn't help you?" McCaney asked, smirking. "With a name like Killa Mike, hell, you shouldn'ta needed no help." The detectives burst out in laughter.

"Nah. They ran and jumped in da car when some more niggas from da South Side gang showed up outta nowhere with guns."

By then, everybody, including Killa Mike, was laughing.

"Dat shit was crazy, man. Those niggas was chasing EB's car, firing automatic weapons and nines and shit. It was like da wild Wild West, cuz. Shit was wild as a muthafucka, cuz."

"What happened then?" Prator asked.

"Shit, I had ta walk home."

"What time you get there?" McCaney asked.

"Man, I don't know exactly what time it was. A nigga like me don't keep up with time. But if I had to guess, I would say about six o'clock, maybe a little before or after, hell I don't know, man. My crew was there waiting on me. I told them I understood why they broke out and shit, and I told 'em, too, how fucked up it was, feel me? I got mixed emotions about dat, you feel me? Anyway, they drove me to da liquor store on Bradfield and Alondra. EB bought three forties of Olde E and a pack of Kools. It was about four-thirty when they dropped me off at da crib."

"What you do then?"

"I laid down on da couch and fell asleep watching rap videos. At six my mama woke me up and said dat sumpin happened at da Bradford house," Michael said. "I looked outside and seen da police cars and crime-scene tape."

"And you had nothing to do with her murder," Mc-Caney said.

"Hell nah! I liked Mrs. Bradford, she was cool people. Mrs. Bradford came over to my crib a couple times. Da first time she asked me to turn down my stereo, you know what I'm sayin'. I was playin' Tupac, 'Picture Me Rollin',' and it was soundin' good to me. I was feelin' it, cuz, like I feel all-a Tupac songs, you feel me?"

"I feel ya," Prator said and rolled his eyes.

"Anyway," Michael continued, "da next time she came to my crib was when she told my mama she saw me at home when I was s'posed ta be at school. I had dis chick named Recee I'd been tryin' to hit for da longest and she finally said, 'let's do da damn thang.' Man, she fine as a muthafucka, and I hit dat shit every which-a way, cuz. Mrs. Bradford probably heard Recee screamin', and shit, 'cause I was puttin' it down like a real Trojan. My big homie always told me dat if you don't make da girls scream when you hittin' it, then you ain't doin' nuttin'."

"Nobody wants to hear about how you put it down in bed, killa," McCaney said. "Keep talkin', but not about the bullshit."

"Look, I didn't 'ppreciate Mrs. Bradford tellin' my moms my business, but I wasn't mad at her. She was jus' doin' what nosy, big-mouth people do! I didn't hold any grudges on her. To tell you da truth, I don't know who would wanna hurt Mrs. Bradford. If anything, I woulda tried to get wit' her, you feel me? I'm into older women."

"Enough of the bullshit," McCaney said. "So you've never been in possession of a .44 Mag?"

"I borrowed my uncle's .44 Magnum for protection against a few rivals who had it out for me."

"What about the gun EB gave you for drugs?"

"You know 'bout dat? EB told you that?"

"Answer the question," McCaney insisted.

"I sold dat gun to a nigga from Oaks Park named Bay Rob, for twice da amount I paid for it."

"I'm gonna need that gun, Killa," Prator said.

"No problem, Officer." Michael looked around the room and leaned forward. "My mama told me her husband, Daryl, did it."

The detectives stood up. "You can go now. I'll have a unit take you home," Prator said.

After Michael left, Prator and McCaney talked about the interview. "It wasn't that there was something that said definitely that Thomas did not do it," Prator said. "It was that there was no evidence that made me think he was ever in that house: no DNA or fingerprints, no one saw him there."

"You right," McCaney agreed. "Teenagers don't usually make good criminals. They tend to be reckless and leave incriminating evidence behind. The majority of 'em always get caught anyhow. The way the evidence was laid out, April Bradford's murder wasn't like that. It was a calculated crime. A crime that still lead me to believe her husband did it or conspired in it."

Just then an inquiry came in reflecting April Bradford's $60,000 life insurance policy. As might be expected, Daryl, as her husband, was the beneficiary.

Although he had not yet proven it, McCaney checked a box on a form that indicated the beneficiary was implicated in the death.

# Chapter 28

## *On the Forensic Front*

Results continued to dribble in on the forensic front. Gunshot residue on Daryl's hands came in as negative.

"What do you mean, negative inconclusive?" McCaney asked.

"Gunshot residue test results can be divided into three categories: Those where residue is found on the clothes. Those where residue is found on the evidence, and those where only morsel amounts are found on the clothing. In this particular case, the last applies," explained Medical Examiner Rhonda Cleveland.

"Right," Prator said. "And we haven't recovered the weapon."

"Which makes it more difficult. You see, when a pattern of gunshot residue is found on a submitted article of clothing and the questioned firearm and ammunition are known, firearm examiners will try to bracket the muzzle-to-garment test results within a minimum and a maximum distance," Cleveland explained.

"I get that," McCaney said.

"But what we're looking for are trace amounts of residue from your suspected shooter. Bring me the gun and I'll talk to you more," Cleveland said.

"What about residue on Bradford's hands?" McCaney asked.

"Once a gun is fired, the gunpowder explodes, which produce high levels of gases at massive pressure that force the bullet from the firearm. Residue from the blast will be undeniably left on the hands of the trigger puller and the victims attire. Despite how small the residue particle is it will have conclusive indications," Cleveland explained.

"This much, I know," said Prator.

"Mr. Bradford's test were inconclusive, however there is a new test, which uses a technology called solid phase micro-extraction combined with gas chromatography, focuses on chemical compounds present in that ejected material. I'll run those test and get back to you in a couple of days," Cleveland said.

"What about the blood in the drain?" Prator asked.

"The blood in the stopper was too small and the blood on the shirt found in the laundry room came back as Mr. Bradford, not Mrs. Bradford," Cleveland explained.

"Could he have cut himself breaking the door glass?" McCaney asked.

"It is possible, but according to the records he had been examined for cuts before he was interviewed, so it was just as likely that the blood came from cutting himself while shaving. Sorry I couldn't be more help to you," Cleveland said.

As Prator and McCaney left the lab, there was one question that they both had in mind. "Where does that leave us?" Prator said out loud.

"We got the same thing that we had when we walked in there, that's what we got," McCaney replied.

"Then what we got is nothing. Nothing but your gut, Mac," Prator said, and tapped McCaney on his stomach.

"That's enough for me."

"But not enough for the DA," Prator said.

"So what now?"

"Let's talk to Anna Sims again."

"Good idea. I got the feeling that she knows more than she's sayin'."

"You think everybody is hiding something, Mac."

"Well, ain't they? Don't you think just about everybody got some form of skeletons in their closet?"

"Absolutely not. That assumption is totally unfounded."

"Yeah, whatever. Well, I damn sure do."

"I know you do, Mac; I guess your instinct and your way of thinking has gotten you to where you are today."

McCaney looked at his partner and smiled. "Damn right it did."

# Chapter 29

## *Anna: the Second Time Around*

Prator and McCaney spoke with Anna again, to ask her to come to the station. They both figured and hoped that there was more to know, and kept sensing she wasn't being entirely honest.

At the station, Prator talked to Stinson while Anna waited in a cubicle. Prator suggested that Stinson conduct the questioning, hoping to get an inconsistent statement or perhaps catch her in another lie.

To set up the interview, someone had to make Anna aware of their suspicions. That honor fell to McCaney, who went into the room with Stinson and Anna.

Several officers had described Anna's physical attributes and beauty as "the bomb" and "she's hot," but Stinson's assessment of her differed.

"Her body without question is 'the bomb,' but her face ain't all that; it's average to me. Put it this way: no way in hell could she compete for *Ebony* front page or a *Jet* centerfold."

It was evident, because she had knowingly and shamelessly carried on an extensive affair with a married man, that Anna had no conscience or morals, concluded Stinson.

"You lied to me," McCaney began as usual with a confrontational measure. "Didn't you?"

"I didn't lie," Anna replied, looking him in the eye, but then admitted, "I just didn't tell you everything. That don't mean I lied."

"That's the same as lying," McCaney explained. Acting as if he was furious with Anna for lying, he stormed out of the room, slamming the door behind him.

At that point Stinson took over the interview. He sat down across from Anna.

"Is there anything you would like to clear up regarding your previous statement?" Stinson asked.

"Why in the hell is he so mad at me?" she asked.

"Maybe because he thinks you're not telling him everything."

"I answered the questions he asked me, what more does he want?"

"In our business, if you don't tell us everything you know, it's the same as lying." He gave her a hard stare. "You have something else to tell us. Let's have it."

At first, Anna described what she had already said: that she and Daryl had a casual flirtation in the beginning, which escalated into a sexual affair, which quickly skyrocketed into emotions, care, and concern, which resulted in love.

Then she added a little more information than she had during the first interview.

"Daryl made me feel good, and not only that, he bought me expensive gifts. I did my part by returning the pleasure the way I knew how."

"Things he couldn't get from his wife, I take it?"

"He told me his wife didn't give him oral sex. He said she thought her mouth was too good to give him a blowjob, and that she didn't get real freaky with it in bed."

Stinson leaned forward. "Not like you, huh? I bet you give it to him right."

"Yes, I do. Just the way he likes it. The thing about me is that I'm a lady in public, a bitch in the kitchen, and a whore in bed. I handle my business, and I'm good at what I do. Pleasing my man is a priority and pleasure. Look, he said she was a dead in the bed, and that she just laid there and didn't move when they fucked and acted as if she wanted it to be over before he even put it in. Yeah, it was my pleasure to accommodate him in that aspect, simply because he took care of me."

"Tell me about the drugs."

"Sometimes we did coke to enhance our sex, and sometimes we just got right down to the nitty-gritty and did what we do, which was get real freaky with it. We knew exactly what each other wanted and how we wanted it." She smiled, looking off, and then added, "I haven't ever run across a man who could keep a hard-on while doing coke, without using Viagra, but Daryl, wow, he could go on and on and on; ump, ump, ump; the more he used, the harder he got."

"Sounds like a real stud."

"For real. I mean, I don't mean to talk about the dead, but if his wife would've been doing her job to keep her husband in her own bed, then maybe he wouldn't have been in mines all the time." She silenced herself in deep thought a few moments.

"But, as I told the other detective, sometimes he scared me. He could switch moods right before I got an orgasm. That Dr. Jekyll, Mr. Hyde personality would kick in and he'd pull out of me then jump up mad about something. I'm not a psychic, but I think he was having flashbacks from the military."

Stinson pressed forward. "Did Daryl ever tell you he loved you?"

She smiled. "All the time. Those three words, 'I love you,' are so meaningful, especially coming from him. I loved it when he said it to me. No one has ever said it better."

"So you loved him too, huh?"

"Yes, I did and I still do."

"You know," Stinson said, "one of the things we use to evaluate a suspect is motive. April, as you probably heard, was pregnant by Tyrone Whitsey, Daryl's best friend, which clearly could be a motive to kill his wife. On the other hand, he was in love with you, and . . ."

Anna looked at Stinson silently a moment, and then suddenly smiled. "Yeah, he told me about it after it happened, but I figured all along she was cheating. You see, a woman needs to be touched, and . . ." Anna paused and smiled. "You think he killed his wife to be with me, don't you?"

"What I think doesn't matter, Mrs. Sims; I am only gathering information and trying to sort out facts from hearsay."

To Stinson, Anna sounded flattered that Daryl might love her enough to kill April to be with her. Stinson felt disgusted, but tried not to reveal what he really thought about the proud but sluttish, remorseless woman sitting before him. Still, Stinson felt that she was holding back information.

After the interview, Anna Sims was dismissed. Stinson met with Prator and McCaney to discuss what Anna Sims had revealed.

"Well?" Prator asked.

"It is obvious that Anna Sims has been evasive and not completely forthcoming in this investigation. In my opinion she is still withholding pertinent evidence," Stinson said.

When the dust settled, the detectives still did not have what the prosecutors needed. They had not found a murder weapon they could tie Daryl with. They had motive and opportunity, but no hard evidence.

"Okay, let's take it from the top," McCaney said. "Let's walk through the timeline of April's and Daryl's activities the day of the murder."

Stinson laughed. "Why, Mac? No matter how it goes you're still gonna think that Bradford had enough time to plan and stage the burglar scene."

"He's right, Mac," Prator said. "So let's consider Bradford's account of the rest of the afternoon. If we relied on the times Daryl gave in his statement, April arrived home at three forty-five."

"The only certainty here is from the surveillance video at Jack Rabbit Liquor & Jr Market, where Daryl arrived at four thirty-two," Stinson said.

"That left a forty-seven-minute gap," McCaney added. "Which gives that punk more than enough time to kill his wife and stage that scene."

"I have driven the route from the Castlegate home to the store and estimated that it took ten to twelve minutes," Prator said. "Subtracting the ten or twelve minutes from the forty-seven minutes left more than half an hour unaccounted for."

"That is enough time Bradford to have spent cleaning up before leaving the house," Stinson said, starting to see it McCaney's way.

"The second unexplained period was the span between when Daryl left Jack Rabbit Liquor & Jr Market and arrived at Home Depot," Prator said.

"Based on surveillance tapes from the two stores, the trip had taken him thirty-four minutes. That was excessive for a six-and-a-half-mile drive that Prator made in less than twelve minutes," McCaney added.

"What happened during that additional twenty-two minutes? Where was Bradford? Disposing of the murder weapon? And if so, where?" Stinson asked.

# Chapter 30

## *Daryl and Chris*

## *Twenty-six Hours After the Death of April Bradford*

That night, Chris and Daryl went out to dinner to a Mexican restaurant on Rosecrans Boulevard called El Castillo's. As they sat down Daryl laughed about an undercover police car he'd noticed following him there. Since his latest interview the police had him staked out, waiting to catch him slipping.

There were lots of unanswered questions Chris had for his friend. "Why aren't you cooperating with the police? You not cooperating with the police only makes it seem like you're hiding something," Chris said.

To his friend's astonishment, Daryl replied, "Fuck them and fuck what they goin' through!"

"Don't you want to know who killed April?"

"I know you heard that she was pregnant and the fuckin' baby wasn't mines, so don't play stupid, Chris. The bitch got what she deserved for all I care! She got caught up, and then fucked up! Life goes on, the way I see it!"

Chris looked at the man who had been his closest friend for many years. They had many disagreements in the past as well as different views on numerous things, including political. At times Daryl got on

Chris's nerves, but now, looking into his friend's eyes, Chris wondered if Daryl was actually capable of murdering his wife.

Daryl then claimed that police had it out for him. "That's why I got two new babysitters," Daryl said; and then he began explaining his alibi to Chris. "They got me on video at Jack Rabbit about the time that April was murdered."

"So you couldn't have done it," Chris said and thought about it, reassuring himself that Daryl couldn't be guilty. But even if he didn't kill her, there were still those unanswered questions. "But, man, don't you wanna know who did it?" Chris asked, not understanding his friend's way of thinking.

"Like I said, Chris, the bitch got what she deserved. She dug her own got-damn grave, as I see it. The fact of the matter is that I didn't have a got-damn thing to do with it. Anybody who thinks I did—including your wife, because I know she can't stand me and probably thinks I killed April—they can kiss my yellow ass then go to hell!"

Chris didn't believe what he was hearing. "How could you say some shit like that, man? No one deserves to be murdered, regardless of what they did! If God forgave us for—"

Daryl cut him off. "Miss me with the God stuff, Chris," Daryl said, pointing in Chris's face. "You know got-damn well I'm a atheist! I don't believe in heaven or hell so don't come at me like that! As far as I'm concerned, I'm the God of my world! I'm the one who fought on the front lines in combat, and I'm the one who spent his own got-damn money on that house, and that Lexus and Tahoe. Me, goddammit! Now I said what I said, and it is what it is, Chris! The low-down bitch was fuckin' that illiterate-ass Tyrone behind my back and got caught up; ain't nothin' else to it! I don't know who killed her and basically I don't give a fuck who did it! And let me tell you how stupid she was: she didn't even have sense enough to make the broke muthafucka use a rubber!"

Chris remembered his wife speaking on Daryl's impotence. "Maybe she wanted to have a baby," Chris said. "Have you ever thought of that?"

"Maybe she did." Daryl suddenly dropped his head in his hands and dropped his tone. "She had told me about the baby, man, and . . ." He was about to pour his heart out to his best friend as he sometimes did, but remembering that Chris told his wife everything, Daryl caught himself and changed subjects. "Did the Lakers win last night?"

Chris ignored the question, realizing what his friend was up to, and refused to change subjects, but stayed on point. "You mean she just came right out and told you that she fucked Tyrone and that she was pregnant by him?"

Daryl released a heavy sigh. "Yeah, man, she did. She eased her way into it, you know, but that was the bottom line."

"As far as the police are concerned, that's motive enough for you to have killed her."

"I don't give a damn what they think!" he snapped. "I told you I didn't do it, and that's the got-damn truth!"

"Have they talked to Tyrone yet?" Chris curiously asked.

"Yeah, they did, and he sang like a mockin'bird and told 'em everything, and I mean everything. I should have never let that nigga move in my house. He done fucked up my whole got-damn world, but it's okay; I'll get it back on track in due time."

All of the information he was getting caused Chris a temporary loss for words. But he abruptly snapped back to reality and boldly expressed his views. "You started the whole shit, man, so don't blame it on April or Tyrone."

"What you talkin' about, Chris? Have you lost your rabbit-ass mind, nigga?"

"If you woulda been home every night with your wife and treated her like the queen she was, instead of screwing around with those street women, this shit would have never happened. The devil you know, boy, I swear—"

Daryl cut him off. "What, nigga? You called me a devil?"

"I'm just saying, man; you're unbelievable and have some fucked-up devilish ways. Man, didn't you recognize that it was really you April needed, but because Tyrone was there as a fill-in, she turned to him and confided in him? It doesn't take a rocket scientist to figure that out. This whole damn thing is your fault."

"Ain't this some shit! So now it's my fault that she fucked that nigga and got knocked up, right?"

"Yes, it is. So blame yourself for everything that has happened. You moved him into your house when you were treating your wife like shit and cheating on her. Don't you get it, man? Tyrone was doin' everything you wasn't."

Incapable of accepting the truth, Daryl became offensive. "Fuck you, and watch your mouth, Chris. Don't let your mouth overload your ass! You'll get a serious beat down up in here, so watch your mouth, boy!"

"Man, Regina really gonna think you did it when I tell her about all this." Chris nodded in disgust.

Daryl snapped, "Tell me somethin', man: why in the fuck do you tell your wife every got-damn thing?"

Chris didn't answer; he just looked at Daryl and wondered who the man sitting across from him really was.

"Ain't no way in hell I'd tell my wife every got-damn thing I do or I did. All they do is take what you tell them and use it against you! That's stupid-ass shit, man!"

"What's so stupid about it?" Chris calmly asked.

"It just don't make no sense! Telling your wife every got-damn thing? Your wife might have you by the balls like that, but me? Uh-uh, hell no! I ain't cut out like that."

"How would you handle it?"

"Have you ever heard of not lettin' your left hand know what your right hand is doin'? Man, ain't no way in hell I'll tell any bitch everything, no way in hell, man. I don't even tell my mama everything," Daryl said and laughed a little.

"Why is that, Daryl?"

"It just ain't the right thing to do as a 'real man.' I'm tellin' you, Chris, one day, Gina gon' use shit against you that your dumb ass told her in the past, just watch what I say. If you don't believe me, just make her mad and see."

"I don't think I'm gonna go outta my way to piss Regina off just to prove your point," Chris said.

"Nigga, I bet you she knows how much money you got in the bank, and um, oh, I forgot; henpecked niggas like you don't have separate bank accounts from their wives, right? Everything is joined," Daryl said sarcastically, laughing. "I bet she knows what time you make it home every day from work, she knows when you need ta take a shit, she knows—"

Chris cut him off, standing. "You damn right she does, and she's supposed to! That's why we have a fruitful, peaceful, meaningful, and loving marriage, Daryl."

"You sound like a fuckin' fool, nigga."

"Transparency, honesty, love, and commitment are the elements that hold a marriage together, asshole!"

"Watch who you callin' asshole, nigga."

"A hit dog with howl."

"Fuck you!"

"I thank God that me and Regina are inseparable and don't hide things from one another. If we have a problem, we talk about it; that's the way it should be in a marriage, not all that bullshit you be doing."

Daryl laughed out loud. "Yeah, whatever, nigga. You wasn't sayin' that shit when you was tryin' to fuck Anna, was you?"

"That was a mistake and thank God it never happened!"

"Let me be real with you, Chris, and take heed to what I'm about to say to you. No way in hell can you stop a woman from givin' away her pussy to another man if that's what she wants to do, and you can take that to the bank."

Chris laughed, but he knew Daryl was right about that. "I'll try to remember that."

"April has proven that to me. I gave the bitch the world, man, and she did me like that."

"It's like I told you, Dee, she didn't want all the material stuff; all she wanted was you to show her some love."

But it was like Daryl wasn't listening to a word that Chris had said to him. He continued, "No matter what you do for a woman—I don't give a fuck how much you give her, what you do for her, or how good you treat her—if she wants to give up that pussy, then she's gonna do it. You know damn well I gave that heffa the world, and—"

Chris cut him off. "Obviously, you gave her every-thing but what she wanted and needed. You gave her everything but love, Daryl. Not all women are into materialistic stuff; I guess you know that by now. Some require love and intimacy, and attention, and want their man to be attentive toward them, listen to them with concern, and be compassionate toward them. Those qualities, man, outweigh materialistic things by a landslide."

The comment silenced Daryl, and during that pause, Chris raised another question. "Tell me somethin', man; why on God's earth would you welcome a no-good, jobless snake like Tyrone to live with you and your wife anyway? His own mama put him out, man' that shoulda told you somethin'. A snake will always be a snake, and a leopard never changes his spots."

Daryl dropped his head. "I was just tryin' to help him the same way I'd help you if your wife or mama threw you out in the streets."

"That kind of compassion and unselfishness should've been displayed toward your wife," Chris said with true conviction.

"Anyway," Daryl sarcastically said, wanting to move on and change subjects, but Chris stayed on point.

"That's what I'm talkin' about, man; you act like you don't even care if April's killer is caught. If it was me, I'd wanna find out who murdered my wife and I'd want them caught."

"It ain't gon' bring her back," Daryl replied, as if not even considering the possibility that solving the murders could bring his family and the Mitchell family closure.

Chris nodded. "How inconsiderate and foul can you be?" With that, Chris stood up, threw some money on the table, and then left without saying another word.

Chris walked out of the restaurant, not really believing the conversation that he just had. Once he got inside his vehicle, Chris called his wife and told her about the conversation that he just had with Daryl.

Afterward, Regina phoned Daryl's cousin, Sherry, and also called a friend of hers, this time coming right out and said what she thought.

"I know Daryl killed April," Regina said. "Almost everything he said was a damn lie! Chris met him for dinner tonight."

"What was he talking about?" Sherry asked.

"Chris told me that Daryl showed no interest in finding out who killed April."

"That's some low-down shit."

"And oh, I don't know whether you already heard or not, but Tyrone was the baby's daddy, not Daryl."

The news astounded Sherry. "You shittin' me, girl."

"I wish I was. And check this out; April had told Daryl she was pregnant by Tyrone."

"No shit?"

"No shit."

"Wow," Sherry replied, not believing what she was hearing, but all into the latest gossip.

"That's what I said. When the detective first told me about it, I remembered her telling me before that Daryl couldn't have kids. But behind all the shit that's going on I wasn't even thinking about that shit, you know. I was just concerned about April."

"I know that's right. So it's possible that April's confession about Tyrone triggered Daryl to kill her?"

"Absolutely," Regina replied. "Think about it, Sherry; why else would anybody want to hurt April?"

"Tyrone might have killed her because he didn't want no baby," Sherry thoughtfully said.

"No, I don't think so. The way I see it, a controlling, egotistical asshole like Daryl couldn't accept or live with the fact that his wife had cheated on him and got pregnant by his friend."

"So he'd rather kill her, than to live in shame. Wow; that's scary," Sherry replied in an uneasy, nervous voice.

"Please," Regina said. "That yellow punk will be locked up in a hot minute, girl. He can run but he can't hide, and whatever is in the dark will soon come to light. You can't hide the truth forever, Sherry. Believe me, that asshole is gonna slip and get caught."

Regina told a different story when she was talking to her friend. Regina spoke on known problems in the Bradford marriage, highlighting Daryl's infidelities, but did not speak on April's unfaithfulness. She eagerly told her about the many days and night Daryl spent away from home, allegedly with hookers or his girlfriend, Anna Sims. She did, however, leave out the fact that her own husband had been flirting with Anna.

She had first heard about it through gossip and had then discovered that he had been flirting with Anna in person, through e-mails, and she had even found her phone number in his pants pocket when washing them. She had forgiven her husband and they'd both promised to put that behind them, move forward, and never make mention of it again.

# Chapter 31

## *Necie and Daryl*

Necie called Daryl's parents' house, hoping to speak with him, and he answered the phone. Her plan was simple enough. She would get Daryl relaxed and talking and get him to admit that he killed April.

"What's up, Daryl," she asked with the recorder on, trying to sound casual. "You all right?"

The call appeared pleasant as far as Daryl was concerned. As long as she didn't pry or venture off into things she had no business in, he was okay with talking to her.

As the conversation progressed, Daryl talked about his Lakers and how brilliant Kobe Bryant was but, staying on point, Necie turned the subject to her dead sister, asking if he had ordered April's headstone yet.

"Just ordered it today," Daryl answered. "It's the nicest and most expensive one out there," he boasted.

"I still can't believe she's dead," Necie replied, easing her way back to the subject.

"Me either, sis. Not an hour of the day goes by that I don't think about her. I damn near cry every time I think about her," he lied. "Goin' to Lakers games just ain't the same without her sittin' next to me. She was a big Kobe Bryant fan, too. Did you know that, Necie?"

Necie ignored the question and asked if he had heard anything about the investigation.

"Nah, sis, I ain't heard shit from those lazy-ass cops. If they wouldn't have been focusing on me so much, they probably would have caught who killed her by now."

His words sounded insincere, as far as she was concerned, and did not verify his innocence. She was convinced without a doubt that he was the one responsible for killing her sister.

Staying on point, she pressed forward. "Do you ever call the detectives or police to find out if they found out anything?"

"Hell yeah, I call 'em," he lied again. "But they always tell me the same shit: no progress. Then they start back focusin' on me again, so I stopped callin' 'em."

The truth of the matter was that Daryl had not called to inquire about the progress or try to urge the investigation, nor had anyone in his family.

"Have you asked if there was anything you could do to help move the investigation forward?" Necie asked.

His tone changed drastically. "They ain't gonna do a damn thing but want me to come down to the station and interrogate me again! I'm tired of those muthafuckas fuckin' with me, thinkin' I did it!"

"What low-down person," Necie continued, "could do some shit like that to a pregnant woman?" She was hoping for a semi or full confession, anything to indicate guilt or conspiracy.

So far, her suspect wouldn't bite. Sounding heartbroken, Daryl told his dead wife's sister that he was filled with sadness at not being able to go home and have April waiting for him.

"One thing I still take pride in doin', sis, is wearing my watch she bought me and my wedding ring. As a matter of fact, I ain't took it off yet. They're symbols of my baby and I cherish them so much. And somethin' else; I want you to know that it don't matter who I'm with, I still wear my symbols, proudly, and will never take them off."

"Where there are many words, there are many lies," Necie's father had once told her, and there it was: she had caught Daryl Bradford in a lie. She had read in the paper that pictures from the scene clearly depicted that he wasn't wearing either his wedding ring or watch that night. Both were on the master bedroom dresser.

Necie pressed forward, hoping that one lie would lead to another, or that she could get him angry enough to confess. "Whoever did it," she said, "I hope they get killed the same got-damn way! My sister was pregnant! What insane, immoral coward would kill a pregnant woman!"

Later that night, Necie called the Bradford house again. This time, Brenda answered. As the conversation persisted, Necie cried, saying how she missed her sister.

"I know you miss her, baby," Brenda sympathetically replied. "I miss her too, and I think about her all the time."

When Necie asked if she thought the police would ever solve April's murder, Brenda said that she wished it would be solved, and then added, "I hope you aren't one of those who think Daryl killed her."

Necie did not want to appear disrespectful to her elder; therefore, she swallowed what she truly thought, to keep Brenda talking. "I just can't believe somebody would do that to her," Necie said.

With that, Brenda advised Necie to close her eyes and to think about all the fun that she and April had together as kids. Necie went along with it, just because, and then she asked to speak to Daryl.

Daryl came to the phone and immediately lit into Necie. "Why haven't you been supportive of me, Necie?"

She fired back, "Why haven't you taken a polygraph, Daryl?"

"I think you're up to somethin', you know that?" he insisted. "All of a sudden, you start callin' here all times of day and night. What part of the game is that?"

"Is your conscience bothering you?"

"Fuck you, bitch! I knew you were sidin' with those got-damn cops! In my book, you either with me or against me! The newspaper spread lies about me, the cops spread lies about me, and—"

"Annnd?"

"And my ass, bitch!"

Necie had him hot as fish grease, just like she wanted him. Her father had told her years earlier that people can't think straight or concentrate when they're mad. As far as she was concerned, he could call her all the bitches he wanted. She once again asked why he wasn't helping the police find April's killer.

"That ain't my fuckin' job! Your cop buddies get paid to do that kinda shit, not me!"

"Do you ever want the crime solved, Daryl?" she calmly asked, keeping her composure.

"What difference would it make? You and Chris talk that same stupid-ass shit! That ain't gon' bring April back, don't y'all idiots know that?" Then he said something even more shocking. "April wouldn't want all this confusion and finger-pointin' at me! She'd want us to leave her alone and let her rest in peace, that's what she would want, but y'all muthafuckas around here tryin' to keep a buncha shit goin' on!"

Again, Necie calmly asked about the polygraph, saying that if he took it and passed, maybe the police and her family would accept his innocence.

"Polygraphs don't work," he insisted. "I took a poly-graph before and lied my ass off and passed it, so they don't work! And when I was tellin' the truth, the damn thing indicated I was lyin'! Fuck a polygraph test! April would roll over in her grave if she knew what y'all was up to!"

Necie wasn't moved by any of this. "What I don't un-derstand," she said, "is why you won't just go down to the police station and take it to clear your name."

"Questions have already been answered," he shout-ed. "I answered every got-damn thing those punks asked me! And even if I did take a polygraph and pass it, do you actually think those rent-a-cops will lay off me? Hell no, they won't!"

He calmed himself minutes later and said that his family wanted to give a reward, but had been turned down by the police, which was another lie. *Why does he keep lying?* Necie thought. *If they had offered a re-ward, I would have heard about it. Why lie if you don't have anything to hide?*

"The newspapers keep pointing at you, Daryl," Necie continued.

"I sent facts to the newspapers that backed up the story I told the police, but they refused to run them. They're so damn focused on me, they won't accept the truth! All of y'all assume the worst about me; but that's all right. The truth will set me free one day!" He suddenly began crying. "You know damn well me and your sister was happy; you know that, Necie! I wasn't a perfect husband, I made mistakes along the way, but she always forgave me and we moved on."

Although she knew that Daryl and April were any-thing but happy the last time she had seen them to-gether, it made no sense for her to alienate him any further by disagreeing, and have Daryl hang up. That would just defeat the purpose. She was determined to keep him talking until he confessed.

"I know," she said. "You two had your sweet and sour moments." Necie felt she was getting too soft and off base.

"April was the best got-damn thing that ever happened to me!" he insisted.

That last comment caused her to catch an attitude. "Then why were you fuckin' with all those street bitches if you loved April so much, Daryl? That's what I want to know. And why are you having an open relationship with Anna Sims?" she asked, pushing him to talk, hoping he'd get angry.

When Daryl didn't answer, Necie pushed harder. "I need to know something from you that would ease my mind a little. Something I've been curious about for a while." Necie said. "On Christmas, since you weren't with April, were you out fucking somebody else?"

"What difference does it make!" he snapped, jumping on the defensive.

"It makes a lot of difference to a woman," she said, matching his tone.

"And if I was with another woman on Christmas that don't mean I fucked her!"

"Yes or no!"

The bold, insensitive man spoke out and told the truth. "Hell yeah, I was fuckin' somebody else on Christmas!" He chuckled and continued, "She was fuckin' somebody else too, so don't get it twisted. She wasn't just sitting home like a got-damn saint. Tyrone was up in her Christmas night. Since you doin' your little bullshit investigation about me and your sister, make sure you don't leave this part out!"

Now it was Necie who had no answer. Hearing the truth about her sister's dirty deeds wasn't easy for her to swallow.

Daryl continued his rant. "Your sister didn't know how to suck a dick, or ride a dick, and to make it plain, she didn't know how to please a man sexually! Now put that in your got-damn report!"

Necie still had no comment.

"Oh, you quiet now, huh? Well, let me share something else with you, Necie. I married April because I knew she was a good girl, a girl who came from a good background with a future ahead of her, you feel me? But as far as sex went, trust me, I took her virginity, and she was dead in bed."

"I don't wanna hear this, Daryl," Necie finally said.

"Well, you're gonna hear this shit, bitch. No matter how much I preached to her the importance of a woman satisfying her man sexually, for the sake of the relationship or marriage, no matter how many times I told her how important sexual pleasure was in order to keep her man in her bed, it didn't make a got-damn bit of difference to April. Anyhow, that's where Anna came in. It was just a sex thing between me and Anna at first, no emotions was involved, you know, and then it began gettin' serious. I tried teachin' April how to please me, but she just didn't get it. I emphasized over and over, time after time, how important it was for a wife to please her husband in all aspects of sex, but like I said, she just didn't get it."

Taking everything into account the alleged killer had said, Necie drew a conclusion. "Obviously she pleased Tyrone sexually, wouldn't you say?"

He snapped, "You know what, Necie?"

"What?"

"Fuck you! I know those got-damn detectives told you about that, but fuck you and fuck them, too! Y'all all thought April was a got-damn angel, but she wasn't. She was far from an angel! She was cheatin' too, so she wasn't no better than me! Now the truth is out and everybody now knows that she was a . . ." He caught himself.

"I dare you!"

"My bad, my bad, but you read between the lines and you know the real. Anyway, I got shit ta do, so what the hell you want from me?"

"Go talk to the detectives and clear your name."

"Why should I call the punk police?" His tone changed after thinking a few seconds. "They have nothing."

"You should do whatever you need to do to help them find April's killer."

"Yeah," Daryl said, ignoring Necie. "I give a fuck! As a matter of fact, I bet your sneaky ass is probably workin' with 'em on the down-low, tryin' to prove me guilty! I wouldn't be surprised if you recording this conversation, waitin' for me to slip and say somethin' to incriminate myself."

"You could only say something to incriminate yourself if you did it, Daryl."

"You got the right idea, Necie, but you got the wrong nigga. I don't trust you for one got-damn second. I know you think I killed April, but at the same time you called me and my mother to chit-chat; bitch, do you think I'm some kinda sucka?"

"I don't think that at all, Daryl," Necie said calmly, sensing that he was getting ready to end the call. She wanted to keep him talking, but he was on to her.

"Don't call here no more, bitch, do you understand? Don't call hear no got-damn more, you oil-slick snake bitch!" He slammed down the receiver.

Determined to help the case along, Necie called the house again and Brenda answered. Twenty-five minutes into the conversation, Necie asked a bold and crucial question.

"Did you know that Daryl was messin' around with a woman he worked with named Anna before April got killed? And did you know that he was sleeping with Anna on Christmas and left April home alone?"

"Excuse me?" Brenda said in an unappreciative manner.

"Did you know your son was cheatin' on my sister with a woman named Anna? In fact, he's still messin' around with her; do you know about that?"

Brenda jumped on the defensive. "Then since we're on the cheating subject, I've got a question for you: did you know that your sister was fucking Daryl's best friend, Tyrone, and did you know her baby was Tyrone's and not Daryl's?"

Necie wasn't expecting that kind of response, being that Brenda Bradford was a professed sanctified woman.

Brenda continued, not allowing Necie to speak. "If there is anything else you'd like to discuss concerning Daryl, then I suggest you discuss it with him! People need to mind their own got-damn business!" Brenda said, then slammed down the receiver, thinking, *I know I didn't raise someone who could kill another human being in cold blood.*

# Chapter 32

## *Thirty-two Hours After the Death of April Bradford*

Detective Stinson waited for Anna in the break room at the post office. Stinson then asked Anna to follow him to the precinct to talk to him.

At his precinct, again, Stinson questioned Anna about her relationship with Daryl Bradford. Some of the detectives still felt that the relationship was at the center of the murder of April Bradford, while others were at a total loss and still speculating.

"Did you and Daryl talk about April?" Stinson asked. "About who murdered her, Mrs. Sims?"

"Uh-uh. I've only talked to him on the phone since . . . since she was murdered. I haven't seen him lately."

"Did he say anything about the murder, Mrs. Sims?"

"We haven't talked about her," Anna insisted.

She appeared guarded in her responses, causing Stinson not to believe her. The truth of the matter was that her responses were guarded because she was still a suspect. Anna knew that the police believed she had motive to kill April, or that Daryl had killed his wife to be with her. In either case, she understood that her answers to the detective's questions could determine her future.

"You never asked Mr. Bradford who might've killed his wife, Mrs. Sims? It's hard to believe that the conversation never came up!" He gave her a stern look.

"Like I said, Detective, we didn't talk about it."

"And you expect me to believe that, don't you, Mrs. Sims?" he added.

She frowned, agitated by his tone and insinuation. "Listen, Mr. Detective; I couldn't care less what the hell you believe or don't believe. I said we never talked about it; leave it at that!" she said with an attitude.

Two hours later, Anna was fighting to stay in control of the situation, but due to Stinson's relentless questioning, Anna felt like she was failing. She had told the detective the same answers to the same questions over and over again, only to hear Stinson say, "Let's go over it again, Mrs. Sims." And the condescending way that he said "Mrs. Sims" was like he disapproved of her and her relationship with a married man. Anna tried not to let it bother her, but it did. What people thought of her was important to Anna; it always had been.

After she broke up with her husband, Harvey, she planned to move on and not see Daryl, but it didn't work out that way. The more she saw Daryl, the more they had great sex together, and the more she grew to love him. *You can't help who you love,* Anna thought. *The heart wants what the heart wants.*

"What did you say, Mrs. Sims?" Stinson asked, breaking Anna out of her intense thoughts.

"Nothing. I didn't say nothing."

Stinson let out a little laugh. "That may be the first true thing you said since we've been in here, Mrs. Sims. You're not saying anything. And you need to start telling me something, because when the truth finally does come out, I would hate to see it come down on you, Mrs. Sims."

Anna leaned forward and looked the detective in the eyes. She was tired of his shit and it was beginning to show on her face and in her tone. "Just what do you expect me to say? I am answering all of your stupid, bullshit questions, no matter how many times and in how many ways you ask them. I've got sense enough to know that all you're doing is trying to make me contradict myself or slip up, but that ain't gonna happen."

They had already kept her for hours at the station, interrogating her, speaking ill of Daryl, trying to get her to say, "Yeah, he did it. He did it for me. I told him to kill that bitch so we could be together," when the truth was just the opposite. Daryl made it plain to her that he would never leave his wife.

That was hard to hear and even harder for her to accept. She loved Daryl, loved him with all of her heart and soul. There he was in her bed every day, loving her. Telling her how much he loved her and no matter how many days he spent there, he would eventually get up and go home to April.

Many a day she would stand in the doorway and watch him drive off and wonder how April could let him in the house after he had been with her for three days. She wondered what kind of a woman would stand for that. Truth was that she hated April and everything about her; everything she stood for. It was April who kept Daryl's profound and faithful love from her, and for that Anna hated April's guts.

"I'm gonna keep asking until you tell me what it is that you're not telling me, Mrs. Sims," Stinson said as if he could feel the hate oozing out of her pores.

"I don't know what you're talking about," she replied as if she was angry.

"Yes, you do, Mrs. Sims. You know exactly what I'm talking about," the detective pushed.

"I'm sure I don't," Anna said but she had a good idea. If she told the detective that she hated Daryl's wife, it would reinforce what she knew the detectives would consider a compelling motive for murder.

"I've been doing this a long time, Mrs. Sims. Long enough to know when somebody isn't telling me everything that they know. And that's you, Mrs. Sims. There is something that you're not telling me. And whatever it is, is important to the outcome of the case. So important that you're guarding it with everything you got."

Anna knew exactly what he meant and knew he was right about her. She laughed and went on to say she was unsure of herself and seeking flattery when she flirted with two married men despite what the end result could be. She continued to minimize the importance of her relationship with Daryl, like it meant nothing to her. She described sex with him by saying, "It was the bomb! Daryl was the kind of lover who will make a woman wanna jump up and grab the chandelier. Ump, ump, ump."

"So it was just sex, Mrs. Sims?"

"The relationship," Anna said, "escalated to a lot more than a flirtation, but the bottom line was that Daryl was in love with April without question."

"Did you kiss Chris Jenkins while you were flirting with Daryl Bradford?"

Anna smiled, as if she was reminiscing about that particular moment. "Yes, I did," Anna responded.

"Wow," Stinson said. "You certainly don't mind putting yourself out there, do you, Mrs. Sims? I guess that's something you take pride in doing."

"Fuck you, nigga," was what Anna's eyes said, and Stinson clearly read the message, but ignored it and continued pressing forward.

"Tell me, Mrs. Sims, how did you feel, having sex with a married man?" Stinson asked. "And how do you feel now?"

"What you mean?"

"I mean with all the chaos going on now in your life. Being a suspect in Mrs. Bradford's murder, being interrogated several times, all that's going on."

"I know I didn't do it, so it don't really bother me."

"Do you feel any different about him now, knowing that he is a suspect for killing his wife and her unborn baby?"

Anna copped an attitude. "First of all, that wasn't his baby! Daryl can't have kids." She waved a finger to emphasize her point. "And secondly, he made me feel good in bed. Let me ask you somethin'; have you ever had sex with a married woman who made you feel so good that you would put up with anything?"

Stinson didn't answer her question, but he knew the answer was yes. But that was a long time ago, before he saw the light and the error of his ways. But none of that was her business.

"I think this will go better if you let me ask the questions, Mrs. Sims."

Anna laughed. "I knew you wouldn't answer the question," she said and smiled. "I can see it in your eyes that you know that feeling. But to uphold your image you won't tell the truth about it."

"Obviously, Mrs. Sims, you're not taking this seriously! I will arrest you right now and throw you in a cell right now for murder. Don't fuck with me!"

"Sorry, Detective," she disingenuously said. "I promise it won't happen again."

Anna understood that she had gotten under his skin and that she needed to be careful just in case the detective wanted to make good on his threat.

"Good. Now answer my question. Do you feel any different about him now, knowing that he is a suspect for killing his wife and her unborn baby?"

"No."

"Why is that?"

"Because I know he didn't do it."

"How? How do you really know that, Mrs. Sims?"

"Daryl ain't that type of man. He loved April. He wouldn't have killed her."

Stinson flipped through his notes. "Let's talk about the statement you made in one of your previous interviews. You said that three days before April Bradford's murder, Daryl said he was falling in love with you?"

"I couldn't control how he felt about me," Anna replied. "And I didn't tell those detectives that I told him that my feelings were mutual for him in my statement. They forced me and tricked me into telling them that Daryl told me he loved me three days before April was killed."

"And yet you signed and initialed every page of your statement. Are you saying that Detective McCaney just made those words up?" Stinson asked.

"I'm saying he twisted them to make them say what he wanted them to say. That's what all you cops do!"

"There were no discussions of divorcing April, were there?" Stinson asked.

"No," Anna agreed. "Daryl never said anything like that."

"What other option was there that would allow you and Mr. Bradford to be together?" Stinson asked. "Was the reason Daryl didn't talk of a divorce because he was already planning to murder April?"

"How would I know what he was thinking?"

"Come on now, Mrs. Sims," Stinson said.

She rolled her eyes. "Then I guess you know, since you know everything," Anna sarcastically said. "Look, am I under arrest or what?"

"No, Mrs. Sims, you're free to go anytime you want," Stinson said.

Anna got up and headed out the door.

# Chapter 33

## *Tyrone*

Tyrone sat in the back seat of the police car, thinking. *Yeah, we'll see who gets the last laugh, nigga. I swear you will, Daryl! I shoulda jus' took my heat to you mama's house and shot your punk ass in the head three times like you shot my woman! But I'm gon' get you, nigga, that's a promise! Every dog got his day, believe dat. Lights out, Daryl Bradford; I'm gon' cancel your contract, ol' bitch-ass nigga! It's goin' down!*

Tyrone had gone as far as stashing a 9 mm pistol in the bushes that surrounded the Bradford home. He planned to take out Daryl. He had already accepted the consequences of death or prison for the rest of his life, and was okay with it, as long as he took out the man responsible for killing his woman and their unborn child.

Earlier that day, he had gone to the Mitchell home to offer his condolences and maybe even get some sympathy for the murder of April Bradford. *Our child, my woman.* He felt like he was a part of their family now and would be accepted as such. After polite introductions they stared disapprovingly at the man, allegedly through proven DNA evidence, said to be the father of their grandchild. Typically, under ordinary circumstances, the Mitchells would have wanted to talk to him and get to know him, but unfortunately, they only offered condemnatory thoughts based on their perception and the situation.

"Oh, my God!" Kathy Mitchell had said out loud, wild-eyed as if she'd seen a ghost. "What on earth was wrong with April when she made the conscious decision to fuck him? Was she on dope or somethin'? I can't believe she even considered fuckin' a man who looks like that! Pants hangin' all off his ass, lookin' mean with those beady eyes, like he's mad at the world, walkin' with that slow, thug walk like he's tough or something; what the hell was wrong with my daughter?"

Stanley Mitchell was shocked as well. "What the fuck!" Mr. Mitchell said out loud. "My baby had sex with him? You mean, this man was gonna be the father of my grandson? Was my baby on drugs and I just didn't realize it? I thought she had more class than that! I'll be got-damned! Walkin' in here all slow and shit, like he's bad! I'll whip yo' got-damn ass, boy! I don't understand for the life of me why my baby had sex with a nigga who look like that! If she was gonna cheat, then goddamn, she coulda found somebody worthy and had a little class about 'em! I swear, these kids these days, I just don't understand 'em." He nodded in disgust. The continual hard stares of disapproval displayed by the Mitchell family toward Tyrone caused him a great deal of un-easiness, which led him to leave almost sooner than he arrived. Fortunately for the detectives, having no knowl-edge Tyrone was inside the home, he walked right into their arms upon departure.

"Tyrone Whitsey," said the officer, looking into Ty-rone's eyes.

"Yeah, what up?" Tyrone replied.

"Detective Prator would like a word with you," the officer said, and then escorted a nonresistant Tyrone to the squad car.

Once he was at the station, Prator wasted no time getting right to the point. "Tell me again about your relationship with Daryl Bradford during childhood and on into adulthood."

Tyrone cleared his throat. "Where do I start," Tyrone said. "Let me start by sayin' this: I dropped outta school in junior high, so I don't know all those big words y'all be usin', but dat don't make me stupid, you feel me? I'm gon' tell it like it was and like it is, da way I know how, so I hope y'all understand me."

"That's what we want you to do," Prator said.

"So stop fuckin' around and answer the man's question," McCaney said.

"Daryl was cool in elementary through high school, you know what I'm sayin'," Tyrone said. "But he had changed when he first came back to da hood after military trainin'. I think he called it boot camp or sumpin like dat. Anyway, he had changed for da worse. It was like he'd gone off to college and came back wit' a master's degree in stubbornness and arrogance. He just wasn't da same Daryl I grew up wit'."

"In which ways had he changed?" Prator asked.

"He thought he better than everybody else in da hood 'cause was in da military. He started talkin' down to people he grew up wit', like me, and a whole lotta more people. He came home braggin' 'bout how many Oriental women he had sex with in da Philippines, Japan, Korea, and other places I can't pronounce. He bragged about bein' promoted to a sergeant and about how he was in charge of a squad of bad boys, as he put it. Bragged about how many people he killed, includin' kids and old people; he just wasn't da same Daryl, you know."

"Well, if he had changed so much, why did you go to him when you needed a place to stay after your mama put you out?" Prator asked.

"And just how fucked up do you gotta be that your own mama put you out?" McCaney asked, barely able to hold back his laughter.

"Mac!" Prator said, giving his partner a disapproving look.

"I'm just saying. You gotta be pretty fucked up to make you mama say get out," McCaney said. He thought that they were wasting their time talking to Tyrone. McCaney was sure he wasn't the killer and he was sure who it was. On top of that, he had no respect for Tyrone.

"You got to excuse my partner," Prator said. "Just answer the question. Why'd you stay at his house? It's obvious that you didn't like the guy."

"Now don't get me wrong, 'cause I appreciated him lettin' me stay at his crib when my moms put me out. Dat showed he still had heart for me, but what I didn't 'ppreciate was when he made April cry. I hated him for dat and I hate him even more now! He came home a few days a week and da rest of his time he spent with his girlfriend, Anna. And when he did come home, he would talk crazy to April like she had been doin' somethin' wrong."

"But she was doing something wrong," McCaney said. "She was fuckin' your worthless ass."

"Dat was way before me and her started messin' around!"

"Still, what kind of friend are you? Man takes you in off the streets, 'cause he still had heart for you. And how do you repay that, but by fuckin' his wife?"

He looked at McCaney and continued, "It was what it was. If he woulda been home wit' his wife instead wit' Anna or one of his other sluts, none of this shit woulda happened!"

"No, Tyrone, this shit happened because you stuck your worthless-ass dick in another man's wife. He found out about it and he killed her for it," McCaney said with an attitude.

"Mac!" Prator shouted again, giving his partner that same critical look.

"Fuck that!" McCaney shouted. "I'm tired of this worthless punk sittin' there like he the fuckin' victim. Shit, it's his fuckin fault that she's dead." He pointed at Tyrone. "You're the reason she's dead, you piece of shit!"

"No, I ain't! He yelled at April all da time for nuttin'!" Tyrone yelled at the detective. "He cursed her out for no reason when he came home at two, three, in da mornin'! He treated his wife foul, and I hate his punk ass for dat!"

"So you fucked her. You thought the thing to do after you witnessed him accuse her of cheating on him was to help her cheat on him?" Prator asked.

"It wasn't like dat. No . . . no, wasn't like dat at all. Me and April talked about any- and everything, you feel me? We played spades and dominoes and tonk, we listened to music, we sang love songs, took strolls to da park every now and then. I really miss dat."

"You romanced her," McCaney said quietly.

"I was feelin' her and she was feelin' me, dat's all it was to it. Then one day while we was playin' cards and talkin', outta da blue, we kissed. From dat day on, we let it do what it do and did what lovers did, you feel me? Secret lovers, dat's what we called it, but to tell you da truth, neither of us didn't like da secret part. Anyway, one day she told me she was pregnant. I was happy about it at first until I started thinkin' about explainin' to everybody how it happened. I know da baby was mines, because she told me dat Daryl hadn't hit it in almost a year and I had been hittin' it damn near every day, you feel me. We started makin' plans, you know;

plans for us to raise our baby, and plans to get da hell away from Daryl. April said she was gon' tell him about da baby right away, but I told her not to."

"Why?" Prator asked.

"I felt awkward, you know, bein' dat he let me stay at his crib and I fell in love with his wife."

"You wasn't feelin' awkward when you was up in her, was you?" McCaney sarcastically said.

"Anyway," Tyrone continued, ignoring McCaney's sarcasm. "I tried gettin' her to hold off tellin' him, but she didn't listen to me and I got scared and confused and split. Then da next thing I know, I find out she had been shot and killed. Wasn't no doubt in my mind who had did it."

"At least we agree on one thing," McCaney said under his breath. "Can I talk to you for a minute, partner?"

"Sure." Prator got up and followed McCaney out of the interrogation room. "What's up?"

"Just wondering how long we're gonna waste our time with that piece of shit? He ain't got nothing to tell us. We just need to go to the DA and give her what we got."

"I just wanted to see if he was gonna change his story. He had just as much reason to kill her as the husband," Prator explained.

"How you figure?"

"He just told you. She wanted to tell Bradford right away and he asked her not to, but she went ahead and told him anyway."

"Yeah, I heard him, and—"

"She's been with this asshole all these years and hasn't left him. Now, she was going to up and leave him for what?" Prator laughed. "For this guy?"

McCaney laughed. "I see what you mean."

"So maybe he wanted her to leave and she told him no, or maybe he wanted her to abort the baby and she said no. The guy is full of shit, *you feel me?*" Prator said, mocking Tyrone.

"Yeah, partner, I feel you," McCaney said. "Okay, let's see where this goes."

For the next hour, the two detectives pressed Tyrone on that point. "You could have killed her yourself," Prator said.

"You got me twisted, homie. I couldn't kill her, I loved her. April was my world, man. She was my everything, you feel me? She changed my life, and—"

McCaney cut him off. "Enough of the bullshit," McCaney said. "Your life ain't changed worth of shit, Davis. You're full of shit!"

"Dat's what y'all think, but I'm tellin' you dat April made me feel like a new man. I hadn't neva' read da Bible, 'cause I didn't know how ta read, you feel me, but she was teachin' me. Man, she was—"

McCaney cut him off again. "So you loved her, huh?" McCaney said, showing his contempt for Tyrone.

"Yeah, I loved her. How many times I gotta say it?"

"And you two wild and fascinated lovers were gonna have a baby?" Prator asked.

"Dat's right."

"How were you planning to support your woman and y'all new baby?" Prator asked.

"I was gonna get a job," Tyrone said sheepishly.

McCaney laughed. "Bullshit! Your sorry ass ain't never had a job in you worthless ass life. And now all of a sudden you were gonna get one, and can't even read enough to fill out an application."

"April was gonna help me, she said she was."

"Easier for you to kill her, Tyrone," Prator said.

"Hell no!" Tyrone yelled and swore to the detectives that he wouldn't have killed April Bradford, but they pressed on.

"You were afraid of Daryl weren't you?" Prator asked.

"I ain't scared of nobody," Tyrone claimed.

"Really? But you let him talk to you like a piece of shit and threaten you," Prator said. "He even hit you once, as I recall, and you didn't do anything about it."

"Dat was different."

"That's why he killed her," McCaney said. "He killed her so she wouldn't tell that crazy-ass Bradford that you fucked his wife. Ain't that really what happened?"

"Y'all can say what y'all wanna say, and think what you wanna think, as many times as you want to, but I didn't kill my woman. Man, y'all on dat dumb shit."

# Chapter 34

## *The Breaks*

Detective Prator needed something to break his way, something that might allow him without question to put a .44 Magnum in Daryl Bradford's hands.

Tips filtered in from different sources. Some of them were good, while some others were just a complete waste of time. Still, every tip, every lead had to be followed up on to see if it would bear fruit.

They went and talked to Denise Mitchell, known as Necie, to speak of the last time they were together, when April appeared deeply unhappy and troubled in her marriage to Daryl Bradford.

"When you and April were together on her birthday, did you see or did she tell you that Daryl gave her a present?" Prator asked.

"No. In fact, she cried because he didn't give her anything, nor did he even acknowledge her birthday by telling her happy birthday," Necie said.

By the time Necie got finished talking, she had painted a picture of Daryl's coldhearted attitude toward his wife. Then Necie played one of the tape-recorded conversations she had with Daryl. As Prator and McCaney looked at the crime scene photo of Daryl's jewelry, including his wedding ring and watch, Daryl was heard saying he had his wedding ring on at the time of the burglary.

Even though Necie had proven that Daryl Bradford was a liar, there were other parts of the recording that Prator had questions about.

"You agree with Bradford that they were happy."

"They weren't close to being happy," Necie countered.

"It was an effort to get him to say something you could use against him," McCaney suggested.

With that, Necie agreed. "Yes, I was. That's not a crime is it?" she said, answering a question with a question.

"Have you ever heard of entrapment?" Prator asked and laughed at the wanna-be detective.

"Gimme a break," she replied. "That nigga killed my sister, I know he did."

The detectives dropped by and spoke to Anthony Hicks. They had meant to talk to him, but there was always some more promising lead to follow up on.

"I saw a car I had never seen before speeding through the neighborhood late that afternoon," Hicks told the detectives.

"That's strange. I've talked to several of your neighbors and they said that they had walked by the Bradford house, or driven by that afternoon and seen or heard nothing," Prator said.

"Hey, I'm just telling you what I saw," Hicks said.

One impression Hicks and the other neighbors agreed on was that Bruno was a highly protective animal. Hicks appeared to be trying to paint a picture of his neighborhood being crime infested, but others described it as quiet and Neighborhood-Watch protected.

The detectives listened as Hicks recounted the events on the evening. When he was done, Prator made the following observation: "Something's not making any sense."

"What's that?" Hicks asked, and smiled a little.

"After Daryl pounded on your front door, why didn't he wait for you?"

"I don't know. Maybe he was excited and in a hurry to get back over there."

"You came out and followed him, offering help, right?" McCaney asked.

"That's right."

"But instead of taking the dog inside with him, where it might confront the alleged burglar, Bradford left Bruno in the backyard, which clearly made no sense."

"Daryl was frantic that day. He wasn't thinking straight."

"While Bradford ran toward the house and you followed," Prator began, "did the name 'April' ever come out of Daryl's mouth?"

"No," Hicks honestly answered.

"Have you ever asked yourself why Mr. Bradford made no mention of his wife's name, Mr. Hicks?" McCaney asked.

The implication was that he didn't shout out his wife's name because he already knew April was dead.

As the day wound down, the detectives finally got a break when receiving a call from Ray Martin, who had responded to the media alert for any information about seeing Daryl Bradford's Tahoe the day of the murder.

"That day," Martin began, "a little after five P.M., I saw that Tahoe at the intersection of Long Beach and Greenleaf."

Prator leaned over and whispered to McCaney, "That's when Daryl said he was traveling from Jack Rabbit Liquor & Jr Market to Home Depot."

Fixated on Bradford's attractive Tahoe, Martin described it down to the shade of blue, tire size, and the type of rims.

One that showed promise was a tip from an old friend of the Bradford family, who suggested that Mc-Caney contact Elliot Phillips, a high school friend of Daryl's brother Dino. When McCaney and Prator paid him a visit, Phillips at first seemed reluctant, but finally cooperated.

That evening, Phillips's phone rang, but he didn't pick up and let it go to voice mail. When he did check his messages he found that Dino, who he had not heard from in years, had left a message, saying, "Let me make myself real clear; my brother Daryl never owned a .44 Magnum. That's all I'll say for now."

Feeling uneasy about Dino's word choice and tone, Phillips reported the call to Prator.

Elliot Phillips described the Bradfords as his childhood second family. It appeared evident that he did not want to say or do anything against Daryl, but when pressed by the detectives, he knowledgeably discussed his encounters with the Bradford family and guns.

"When we were younger, me and the Bradford brothers used to hang out," Phillips said.

"What would you gentlemen do when you got together, Mr. Phillips?" Prator asked.

He paused and looked at the two detectives, as if he was deciding how honest he was going to be with them. "Sometimes we would take our fathers' guns without permission and fired them for kicks."

"Where would you fire these guns?"

"In our backyards, at riverbeds, in parks, and sometimes even in the alley that led from Castlegate to Washington Street," he said.

"Let's cut to the chase; have you ever known Daryl Bradford to have a .44 Magnum in his possession?" McCaney asked.

"Yes. I've seen Daryl with a .44 Magnum, and I've seen one at the Bradford household before."

McCaney looked at his partner, silently saying with his eyes, "I told you so!"

"And you're sure about this?" Prator asked.

"Yes, sir, all three Bradford brothers owned .38 Specials and .22 pistols. Mr. Bradford was one of those gun freaks, you know. Called himself a gun enthusiast. He had a whole cabinet full of different types of guns."

"You say that they owned .38 Specials and .22s; where did Daryl get the .44 that you saw him with?"

"I never did ask Daryl where he'd gotten the .44 Magnum from. It wasn't my business."

"But you're sure you saw Daryl Bradford with a .44 Mag?" McCaney pushed.

"Yes, sir. Without question."

McCaney turned to his partner.

"I think we got what we need," Prator said.

# Chapter 35

## *The Arrest*

The FBI lab completed a report listing individual pieces of evidence Bonner and Prator had submitted from the April Bradford murder case, including a jogging suit belonging to Daryl found in the master bedroom and a pair of his tennis shoes recovered from outside the back door.

The report titled "Results of Examination" read:

During the discharge of a firearm particles are produced. These particles are from the mixture of most cartridges and can be deposited on surfaces in the vicinity of discharging a firearm, including clothing worn by the suspect and shooting victim. Gunshot residue particles were detected on Daryl Bradford's shirt, pants, jacket, and tennis shoes.

When receiving the report, Prator began making phone calls.

Close to the same time, Stanley Mitchell made a call to his friend Ronald Hawkins, the chief district attorney, arguing that his daughter's murder had been mishandled, and that if the DA's office refused to prosecute Daryl Bradford he would get on the World Wide Web and tell everyone about April's murder and how they had ruined it. Immediately, Hawkins summoned his chief assistant DA, June Johnson. As his star prosecutor, and not wanting the media to get a hold of anything that could potentially damage the reputation of the office, Hawkins suggested that Johnson make the Bradford murder case her priority. She had handled high-profile murder cases, often using controversial and highly effective tactics, causing her to come out on top. Defense lawyers described her as a magnificent and extreme lawyer, someone who "pushed the limits," and her methods as "over the top and beyond the call of duty." People were so impressed, she was featured in a magazine, and a Hollywood producer had pushed for a television reality show based on her life, but she declined the notion before it gained any serious traction.

Called by some a "drama queen" in the courtroom, Johnson, who was head of the DA's special crime unit, was known for her ability to mesmerize jurors by animatedly and impressively demonstrating her theories on a case. Perhaps her most controversial trick was used in the Joe Downey trial, when Johnson tied down and straddled her co-prosecutor on a bloody mattress, then demonstrated with a nine-inch blade her theory on how Downey stabbed her husband thirty-one times.

Inside courtrooms, ADA Johnson thrived on that "Oh my God" moment when the jury finally realized that's how it really happened. Johnson's enthusiasm and determination, she said, came from the words of wisdom her father instilled in her during childhood: "A quitter never wins and a winner never quits. Success is achieved by those who try, and maintained by those who keep trying, with a positive mental attitude!" Those words helped elevate her to the top of her game.

As a prosecutor, Johnson's view was to relentlessly go after those she believed were guilty.

When the detectives, crime-scene investigators, and police department heard Johnson was about to go full-force on the Bradford murder case, they felt relieved and were confident the long arm of the law was about to reel in Daryl Bradford for murder.

After carefully going over the Bradford murder case several times, Johnson met with Prator to discuss his views and findings. Afterward, she was confident she could deliver a conviction.

"We're going to proceed and charge Daryl Bradford with murder in the first," Johnson stated.

Proceeding forward with the Bradford case, Johnson met with a judge and went over the particulars to obtain a warrant for Daryl Bradford's arrest.

She had explained to Prator that the evidence was largely circumstantial; they had no eyewitnesses, no DNA, very little forensic evidence, that only the gunshot residue test could tie Daryl Bradford to the murder.

Prator smiled. "I'd say that's enough for someone of your stature, Attorney Johnson."

"Call me June," she replied. "I certainly hope it is, Detective. My father once told me 'things aren't always what they seem.' Only time will tell about this one."

After a warrant was put out for Daryl Bradford, Prator and McCaney, accompanied by another unit, drove swiftly with their flashing red and blue lights toward the Bradford residence. When they approached the Bradford home, Daryl was pulling into the driveway. McCaney had opened his door before Prator even stopped the vehicle, stormed out of the car, and aggressively approached Daryl, who was still sitting inside his vehicle.

"You thought you got away, didn't you, slick?" McCaney angrily said, opening the car door. "I told you I was gon' bring your oil-slick ass down, didn't I? Get the fuck out." McCaney yanked Daryl Bradford out of the vehicle and cuffed him. "You're under arrest!"

"What the fuck is this?" Daryl yelled. "Unloose these damn cuffs before I sue you!"

"Fuck you!" McCaney said. "I should fuck you up right here, coward!"

"Kiss my ass, you damn rent-a-cop! I'm gon' sue the whole damn department; then I'm gon' sue both of y'all bitches! Y'all fuckin' with government property, you understand? Just wait 'til I finish with y'all mutha-fuckas! I guarantee both of y'all bitches will be in the welfare line when I'm done!"

McCaney wanted to bust him in the mouth, but there were too many law enforcement witnesses who would snitch him out to IA; but that didn't stop him from manhandling Daryl and throwing him into the back seat.

On the way to the jail for booking, Daryl didn't an-swer any questions, but instead, continually said, "I need ta talk with my lawyer. Call my lawyer from your cell phone, will you? I need to talk with him!"

Prator read him his rights. "You have the right to remain silent. Anything you say or do can and will be held against you in a court of law. You have the right to speak to an attorney. If you cannot afford an attorney, one will be appointed for you. Do you understand these rights as they have been read to you?"

"I understand that I need to talk to my lawyer."

"Do you know what this is about?" Prator asked.

McCaney jumped in before Daryl could respond. "Hell yeah, he know what it's about, that's why he ain't sayin' shit! Just like I said from day one, he's guilty as sin and he's goin' down! We gotcha, slick."

Daryl, not able to contain himself any longer, finally responded. "I don't know what this shit is about, but I do know what's gonna happen to y'all as an end result, believe that. But since y'all seem to have everything all figured out, then tell me what this is about, will you?"

"You're under arrest for the murder of April Bradford," Prator said.

Daryl nodded as if he was stunned. "Seriously? You
bullshittin', right?" Daryl replied. "How many times do
I have to say that I didn't kill April?"

McCaney frowned. "You ain't so slick no more, are
you? Life's a bitch and now you busted! You know
what, Bradford; jail is too good for people like you. I
hope you rot in hell for what you did to your wife and
your best friend's baby!"

"Kiss my ass!"

"By the way; I've got a few words of advice for you.
If the soap drops while you in the shower, don't pick it
up," McCaney suggested, laughing. "Never smile, walk
slow, and always beware of your surroundings. Baby
killers fall in the same category as rapists and child
molesters; don't forget that, either," McCaney added.

"You talk tough shit hidin' behind that badge, don't
you?"

Prator jumped in. "Enough of the bullshit."

Daryl invoked his right to an attorney and refused to
answer questions. After he was arraigned and charged
with murder, his lawyer, Willie Starks, a razor-sharp,
high-dollar lawyer from Indianola, Mississippi, con-
tacted a bail bondsman and Daryl was released on a
$250,000 bond.

When Daryl and his family gathered in Starks's office, the attorney candidly laid out the case as he saw it,
giving his thoughts on how he would present the case
in a courtroom.

"We're going to exhibit the truth," said Attorney
Starks. "I have to proceed with this case as it is. We've
got to take into account that the folks on the jury will
dislike Daryl off the bat. I'm sorry to say, Daryl, but you
have a reputation as a bully, and I'm certain the DA will

have many to attest to that. Your unfaithfulness with April will come up. Your affair with Anna at the time of the murder will come up and taint you; none of this makes you a model citizen. The deck is stacked against us," Starks explained, and continued, producing a sliver of optimism.

"I would lay that out to the jury, and then explain that April was also engaged in her own infidelities. I would explain the details of her pregnancy and remind jurors that her unborn child was conceived outside of the marriage. I'm certain her parents will not appreciate me labeling their deceased daughter a slut, as the jury will characterize her, but it is what it is. The best thing we got going is that there is no concrete evidence that you committed a murder. Circumstantial evidence will not get it done for the prosecution."

After a thoughtful family meeting, the Bradfords, were not impressed by Attorney Starks's words, therefore, instead of straight-out telling him 'you're fired', they let him down easy, telling him that they'd seek further counsel. They didn't want to hurt his feelings, neither did they want to lose friendship with him. They had subsequently hired Perry Brents, a man considered one of the top guns in Los Angeles defense attorneys.

Brents had been a commanding presence in Los Angeles courtrooms for decades, representing defendants in some of the most sensational cases in the State of California. In courtrooms, Attorney Brents was famous for shrinking cross-examinations exhaustive in length. He could be forceful and feisty, and quickly divert to cool, calm, and calculated.

Attorney Brents had a reputation of pounding and pounding away at a witness until he got the results he wanted. He would ask a witness the same question over and over and over, changing it a bit, until he got the answer he needed.

Word quickly spread throughout the Los Angeles and Compton courts that Perry Brents had been hired by the Bradfords to defend Daryl. Many in the legal community believed that this was a case Attorney Brents could easily win, based on his courtroom extremism, theatrics, tricks, and aggression.

June Johnson was sickened, hearing the news. "Damn!" she yelled from her office chair. Johnson laid her cards on the table, strategizing while considering what facts she was working with. *Circumstantial evidence is all I have!* Johnson thought realistically. *No way in hell can I beat Perry Brents with circumstantial evidence! No DNA evidence, no eyewitnesses, no fingerprint evidence, no ballistic evidence, and the police haven't been able to find the damn murder weapon! The only scientific evidence I have is the gunshot residue test from the FBI, but that got-damn Perry has already filed a motion to keep it out of the courtroom immediately after taking on the case, saying the evidence hadn't been carefully preserved and could have been contaminated. I've gotta figure out a way to beat him and I will not settle for less!*

Rumors rapidly and broadly spread that the extraordinary, popular attorney charged a hefty fee. Some argued that Perry Brents didn't take on the case for the money, that he took it on to hand Johnson a loss in a high-profile case after she had beat him repeatedly in several courtrooms back in the day. It was clear to those who knew their history as rivals that Perry Brents was out for revenge.

At Colin P. Kelly Elementary School the competition had begun between Perry and June, in mathematics tests and spelling tests, they contended to know each of the previous United States presidents, they argued over knowledge of Dr. Martin Luther King Jr.'s demonstrations and treaties.

In junior high, at Roosevelt, the rivalry continued in music class, as the two combatants competed to see who could play the piano, trombone, and saxophone the best, who could write the most touching and meaningful songs, they competed to become class and school president, and ultimately, to prove who was the smartest, who could win the spelling bee, which Perry won by a landslide.

In high school, at Dominguez, the challenge had escalated to a higher level of confidence and skill. While Perry was school president and also in charge of student event planning, president of the glee club and the drama club, was obsessed with gaining popularity and now even a girl, June was already taking online college courses. Coincidently, they had both decided to become lawyers. Hearing through the grapevine about June's advanced studies, Perry began studying three times as hard, determined not to beaten in anything by June.

At Compton Community College and subsequently Dominguez Hills University, the opponents met again, now suited and booted, equipped for courtroom battles in their law classes. Both were articulate, intelligent, eloquent, assertive, explosive, and at the top of their games for the level that they were currently at. As far as they both were concerned, there was no such thing as two good lawyers who stemmed from Kelly, Roosevelt Junior High, and Dominguez High School during the same years; there could only be one. The only difference between the combatants now was that Attorney Brents relocated his firm to Beverly Hills, and June Johnson remained in Compton.

In spite of his confidence and winning record, secretly, Perry Brents, after taking everything into account, had his doubts about the Bradford case. And also, secretly, he somewhat feared losing to June Johnson again. "She's tough," he concluded. "A warrior pit bull in a pantsuit! Watch out, JJ; Perry Brents is in the house and thirsty for revenge by way of a publicized win! I'm coming to get you, you tactful bitch, I'm comin' at you with all I got!" He chuckled at his comment.

# Chapter 36

## *Questioning Daryl*

The following morning, Daryl Bradford returned to the police station, accompanied by his lawyer, Perry Brents. On the advice of counsel, Daryl was respectful and cooperative with the detectives. Brents was able to make Daryl understand that the way he presented himself here would most definitely play a role later.

"Why didn't you have blood on your clothes from kneeling at your wife's side?" Prator asked as the interrogation continued.

"I don't know."

"Mr. Bradford, did you love your wife, April?" Prator asked, pacing back and forth in the interrogation room, while McCaney sat looking at Daryl, smiling.

He dropped his head, as if about to cry, and then slowly spoke. "I loved April with all my heart and soul," he said. "April was my world; she was my other half, my irreplaceable and significant other. There was no me without her. There's no other way to put it."

McCaney wanted so badly to say something, but managed to contain himself.

"Do you really expect me to believe a man can love his wife the way you say you do, while simultaneously being unfaithful to her?" Prator asked.

"I made a mistake," Daryl said, no longer confrontational with the detectives. "I wish I could turn back the hands of time and change the way I went about doin' things, but I can't. I had loved my wife ever since I first laid eyes on her in elementary school. Regardless of the mistakes we've both made during the course of our marriage and relationship, as I said, I loved her unconditionally and she was my world. I couldn't care less who questions my love for her." He glared at the detectives, frowning. "I guess it's easier for some people to believe a lie than to accept the truth."

"Did you still possess that same love for your wife after discovering that she was pregnant by a friend of yours whom you allowed to move into your home?" Prator asked.

"I still loved her the same," Daryl replied. "Like any man would, I admit, I didn't take it well at first, but like always we talked about all of our issues, plans, and indifferences, and found common ground." He paused a moment and then added, "To keep my wife pleased, sometimes I had to bend a little more than I wanted to, but I did what I had to do to keep her happy. That was my obligation. Yeah, I was angry when she told me about everything, mainly because I knew the baby wasn't mines. Like I said, what man wouldn't be angry? But we talked about it, you know, and agreed to go through with it. I promised her I would love the baby just the same as if it was mines. We talked about puttin' the episode behind us and movin' forward as a family."

"Do you have sex with all women you flirt with, Mr. Bradford?"

Brents leaned closer to Daryl. "They're getting ready to ask you about Anna Sims. Just like we talked about," he whispered to his client.

"No, man," Daryl answered. "I do not have sex with every woman I flirt with or who flirted with me."

"The last time we talked, Mr. Bradford, at the time

of the murder, you described your relationship with Anna Sims using the words she did: 'a casual romantic relationship', is that right?"

"What about it?"

"Were you in love with Mrs. Sims at that time?" Prator asked.

"Not at all," he replied. "I told you that me and Anna was just flirtin' around at first and things escalated. When I saw her after work hours, it was just somethin' to pass the time by when me and April were mad at each other and wasn't talkin'."

"Mrs. Sims told us that three days before the murder you told her that you loved her."

"I didn't tell her that."

"I have her signed statement right here," McCaney said and held up a piece of paper. "Mrs. Sims was certain that you said that you loved her three days before the murder of your wife, the same wife you said you loved so much. Explain that."

"I didn't tell her that," Daryl answered. "You're twisting my words."

"So what you're saying, Mr. Bradford, is that Anna twisted your words, right?" Prator asked.

Once again, Brents whispered in Daryl's ear before he answered the detective's questions. The night before, they had discussed the possibility that it may become necessary to throw Anna under the bus.

"Yes; Anna was mistaken by what I said and actually meant. If I did say that it was while we was fuckin'. Hell, I'm sure both-a y'all have told a woman what you know she wanted to hear to get some pussy."

Prator ignored Daryl's true comment, and allowed McCaney to jump in.

"What are the odds that three days after you tell Anna Sims you have fallen in love with her, a burglar breaks in and murders April?" McCaney asked.

"I don't know. I never was much of a gambler, Officer," Daryl replied sarcastically.

McCaney laughed. "No, Bradford, you're a lover, right?"

Daryl didn't answer.

"Are remarks like that really necessary, Detective?" Brents asked, and looked at Prator as if to say, "ask my client a real question."

"How come it took you so long to get home that day?" Prator asked.

"What you mean?"

"I mean it took you twenty-five to thirty minutes to drive a distance usually covered in ten to twelve minutes. How do you explain that?"

"It was because traffic was heavy that day, I guess."

"We got an eyewitness who said he is certain that he saw your Tahoe miles from where you claimed to be at that time. How do you explain that, Mr. Bradford?"

"He was mistaken," Daryl said and Brents nodded his head. In the short time he had, he had coached Daryl well.

"This witness described your Tahoe in perfect detail," Prator said.

"A lotta people drive Tahoes. Maybe he saw one that looked like mine."

"Let's talk about the teenager who lived next door, Michael Thomas," Prator suggested.

"I never trusted the thug. Me and April had problems in the past with him. She tried talkin' to him sometimes in an effort to straighten him out and turn him in the right direction, but you know how teenagers are; they think they know everything and won't listen to words of wisdom or constructive criticism."

"Did you have anything whatsoever to do with April's death?"

"No, I didn't. And if you detectives wouldn't be fo-cusin' on me so much, maybe you woulda found the real killer by now."

"Are you saying, indirectly, that you think Michael Thomas is the person who put a gun to the back of your wife's head and pulled the trigger three times, blowing her face off?" Prator asked.

"Listen," Daryl said. "I don't have a crystal ball, but he is and has always been on my list of suspects. I don't know who killed April, but I can tell you and everybody else who's barkin' up the wrong tree I didn't do it! But I know one thing; you will never find out who killed her if y'all keep tryin' to convict me for killin' her! I admit that I made mistakes durin' our marriage and I wasn't no saint, but got-dammit I didn't kill her!"

"That's what juries are for, Mr. Bradford," Prator calmly replied.

Brents had found out that Michael Thomas had told police that he had stolen his uncle's .44 Magnum and that the same size bullets as the ones used to kill April were found in the Thomas household. He had told Da-ryl what to say if the detectives even bought it up.

"Why would my neighbor have bullets that fit a .44 Magnum and not have the gun? It's real simple," Daryl said, using his own logic. "He hid the gun. He's noth-ing more than a hustling thug who smokes dope and drinks alcohol all day, every day, and hangs with his homeboys, indulging in what low-down thugs indulge in, which is crime. He walks around with his pants han-gin' off his ass all the damn time, and what gets me is that he has on a belt. What kinda shit is that?"

"Nobody asked you to make a statement, Bradford. I'll ask the questions and you answer them," Prator said, but Daryl continued without being asked a ques-tion.

"I'd like to add this: I wouldn't want anyone to be falsely accused of a crime, I know how that feels, but Michael Thomas really needs to be thoroughly investigated, and I mean thoroughly."

For the next half hour, the detectives pushed Daryl on the timeline of events, until they got around to the glass at the back door and the jewelry.

"So you want us to believe that burglars looked at two jewelry boxes and did not take anything?" McCaney said.

"I never said nothing about no burglar; that's the shit y'all cops keep pushing to me," Daryl said.

Brents touched Daryl's hand and he changed his attitude.

"But if you say that's what happened, then that's what happened," Daryl replied.

"Did you really love April for the entire duration of the relationship and marriage, Mr. Bradford?" Prator asked.

"Yes, I loved her; how many times do you want me to say it? April was my world; she was my other half. And now that she's gone, and Lord knows she's gone to a better place, I can't seem to live without—"

McCaney cut him off before he could finish. "Spare us the sermon, Bradford, and just answer the got-damn question yes or no."

"I've already answered the got-damn question."

"Then if you loved your wife so much, if she was your other half as you so eloquently put it, and she was your world, Mr. Bradford, then why did you cheat on her?" asked McCaney in a convicting tone.

"Sex," Daryl said.

"Sex?" Prator asked. "Explain yourself, Mr. Bradford."

Daryl looked at his lawyer and Brents nodded his head. "I'm not good at sugar-coatin' things, but the best way I can put it without gettin' too detailed is that April, and I don't mean no harm to the deceased, but she was dead in the bed. She just laid there like a dead person and didn't move. No oral sex, no excitement, nothin' but—"

"We get the picture, Mr. Bradford," Prator said.

"Did you kill April?" McCaney blatantly asked.

"Hell no, I didn't kill her! How many times do I—"

McCaney interrupted him again. He had grown tired of this and was ready to pull the gloves off. He decided to take a more aggressive approach, this time attacking his manhood.

"You didn't like the fact that your best friend was not only fucking your wife up while you were out fucking Anna, but impregnated her as well, did you, Mr. Bradford, did you?" McCaney didn't give him a chance to answer. "I remember a song by Johnnie Taylor, entitled, 'Who's making love to your old lady while you are out making love.'"

Brents tapped his pen against his legal pad on the table. "Control your partner, Detective Prator."

But McCaney didn't stop. "Obviously, Mr. Bradford, you weren't pleasing April in bed, because if you were then she wouldn't have had to turn to Tyrone Whitsey for sexual pleasure. And by the looks of things, in my opinion, it appears that she pleased him enough to impregnate her, and my bet is that she probably enjoyed it. What do you say to that, Mr. Bradford?"

Remaining calm was difficult for Daryl when he was being attacked, but he and Brents talked about this. Daryl had told him about his confrontations with McCaney and knew that this was coming. Brents just hoped that Daryl could keep his head and not say anything stupid or, worse, something that would come back to bite him in court.

McCaney had dealt with guys like Daryl before and knew exactly how to get underneath his skin and press all the right buttons to agitate the hell out of him.

Daryl surprisingly collected himself and smiled. Since junior high school, he had considered himself as a good lover, and since then he was a self-professed top-notch and skilled lover, knowing exactly what women wanted and how they wanted it.

"If you only knew," Daryl replied, smiling. "I'll put it this way; I hit homeruns, make touchdowns, and knock down three-pointers in bed, so me bein' the cause of April cheatin' is farfetched and not true. The only thing I am incapable of is makin' babies. Trust me, Detective, the rest is all good; you betta ask somebody." Daryl chuckled.

McCaney hated his arrogance and was determined to break him down. "I'm sure April felt that Tyrone Whitsey was all good, too. I think you'd betta ask somebody; how 'bout that, potna?"

Daryl looked at Brents. "Is there a question you want to ask, Detective McCaney?"

"Isn't it true, Mr. Bradford, that you killed April because she betrayed you?" McCaney finally asked.

"How many times do I have to tell you I didn't kill April," Daryl replied, frowning.

"And isn't it true to uphold your image, you had to do what you had to do, because the baby wasn't yours and you knew that once people found out you'd be ridiculed forever?" McCaney was determined to throw everything including the kitchen sink at Daryl Bradford.

"That's a lie!" yelled Daryl. "I told you me and April made plans to keep it and we agreed to—"

McCaney cut him off before he could finish his sentence. "Come on, Bradford. You're as transparent as glass and I can see straight through you. A man of your stature . . . You're an ex-military sergeant. Your wife being impregnated by another man," he said, "would have ruined your image, wouldn't it have, Bradford?"

"It wasn't about my image, it was about—"

McCaney cut him off again. "An ex-sergeant in charge of a squadron, and current government employee, a man of so-called high standards, accepting the reality that his wife fucked his best friend and got pregnant by him; I can guarantee that a man like you wouldn't be able to accept that! That's why you killed her, isn't it, Bradford?"

"I think we're done here," Brents announced.

And with that, Brents and Daryl got up and walked out.

# Chapter 37

## *Killa Mike*

Despite the fact that they had made an arrest in the case and that McCaney was confident that they had the right man, after all that had been said about Michael Thomas, Prator thought he deserved a second look.

After being picked up by uniformed officers and brought to the station, Michael Thomas walked into the interrogation room with a slow, cool swagger; as usual, his pants hung off his butt. The belt he wore served no purpose whatsoever. A judgmental person would say that Thomas was an obvious, worthless menace to society, lacking character, particularly wearing braids, frowning.

"You know you can have your mother or an attorney present for this interview," Prator began.

"Why? I ain't got nuttin' to hide," Thomas said.

"Why did you agree to talk to us?"

"Because I wanted to help Mrs. Bradford any way I could. She was a mentor to me, you know what I'm sayin'. She was cool and she listened to me. I even think she understood me and what I was goin' through."

Prator took his time leading Thomas through the events of the day of the murder, how he had cut classes and spent much of the day out for revenge on someone who owed him money for a drug transaction. Instead of collecting the money he received a memorable ass kicking.

Thomas had been grounded after April told his mother that he had ditched school, yet their investigation showed that there were no mentions of Thomas ever being aggressive. In fact, it was stated that when he did go to class his eyes were tight as an Oriental and red as fire. He would laugh at things, it was noted, that weren't funny, and would soon fall asleep, resting his head on the desk.

"Whenever I saw Mrs. B., she sometimes joked with me, but would always urge me to finish school and afterward pursue an education. She talked to me a lot about how important an education was and how niggas who ain't got an education had ta settle for dead-end, minimum-wage jobs wit' no benefits, and be subjected to strenuous, physical, miserable, endless work, you know what I'm sayin'?"

"What else did you and Mrs. Bradford talk about?" Prator asked.

McCaney sat quietly, thinking that this was a big waste of time.

"She'd preached to me, you know. She be sayin' things like, 'At da rate you're going, Michael, you'll end up dead by da time you're out of your twenties,' or 'You'll end up doing a life sentence in prison. Don't waste your life doing worthless shit!'"

"Is that what she said?"

"Well, Mrs. B. didn't curse, but other than dat, dat's what she said."

"Go on," Prator urged.

"She'd tell me all da time dat you only got one shot; use it constructively, productively, and wisely. 'No one can hold you back or keep you down but yourself, remember dat,' she would always say! 'Bad company ruins good character, remember dat, too. Don't become another statistic, Michael, make your mother proud and make something of yourself.'"

Thomas talked about how April had willingly inserted herself into the youngster's life, seeing he was on a self-destructive path. Thomas appreciated her constructive criticism, regardless that she'd snitched him out many times to his mother.

"What did your mother do about it?" Prator asked.

"My punishment was dat my moms took away da Camry she bought me," Michael replied.

"I bet that pissed you off, didn't it?"

"I didn't really trip 'bout it, you know what I'm sayin', 'cause I had a backup plan. All I did was sneak home durin' school hours and take da car while moms was at work, feel me? Sometimes I even took a late-night ride to scoop up a girl or chill with my homies, while moms was 'sleep. I be thinkin', you feel me? My brain always be goin', thinkin' of shit, 'specially when I done smoked a blunt."

"Mr. Thomas," Prator asked. "Did you have anything to do with the murder of April Bradford?"

"No, sir," he respectfully replied. "Ain't no way I woulda or coulda hurt Mrs. B. She taught me good, positive stuff about how I should live, you know what I'm sayin'? She wasn't doin' nuttin' but tryin' to keep me outta trouble, dat's all she was tryin' ta do, and I respected dat to da fullest. She cared about my future, know what I'm sayin', and like I said, outta respect, I listened to her, even though I really wasn't tryin' to hear dat kinda stuff back then."

"Because you're a thug, ain't that right?" McCaney said, jumping in.

"Hey, I am who I am, I do what I do, and it is what it is. I'm a Atlantic Drive Compton Crip 'til da casket drop, and I ain't tryin' to hide or deny it, you feel me? And like I said, I do what I do."

"And what is that?" McCaney asked, smirking.

"Which is basically hangin', bangin', and slangin'. Blowin' trees and get my drank on, dat's what I do, but ain't no way in hell I coulda killed a pregnant woman, especially one who tried to keep me on da right track and was always preachin' to me how to live right. Dat woulda been like pullin' da plug on my own life-support system, you know what I'm sayin'? She always told me stuff like, what you do in life follows you. Don't go out there and get no felonies on your record 'cause nobody will hire you, stuff like dat, you know what I'm sayin'? Mrs. B. was like a second mama to me, and to tell you da truth, I wish I could have a few minutes wit' da fool who killed her," he said and clinched his fists and held them up. "I'd put these thangs on him real tough, you know what I'm sayin'?"

It took a minute, but McCaney had grown tired of sitting quietly. "Yeah, just like you put 'em on those South Side Crips who beat your ass that day, right? Anyway, you go by the gang name of Killa Mike, right?"

"Yep, dat's me. It is what it is."

"And isn't true that you are actively affiliated with the Atlantic Drive Compton Crips?"

"I jus' said dat, Officer. Atlantic Drive 'til da casket drop."

"So then, Killa Mike, why don't you tell us exactly how many people you have killed to earn the name Killa Mike?"

Thomas smirked. "You trippin', cuz," Thomas said, then he looked at Prator. "Dis fool is straight trippin'."

"You a thug, right?" McCaney pressed on.

"'Til da casket drop," Thomas replied.

"Then answer my question, Killa. Exactly how many people have you killed to earn the name Killa Mike?"

"I ain't got a problem wit' dat, but you got me twisted up in here, cuz. I might not got a degree, but I ain't stupid, either, you feel me."

"What you mean, Killa?"

"You tryin' to get me to incriminate myself, dat's what you tryin' ta do. But it ain't gon' work, homie. You got da right idea, but da wrong nigga," Thomas said.

"Obviously, we know you didn't earn that name by killing flies or roaches or shooting your neighbor's pigeons, so again, Killa, tell me exactly how you killed April Bradford and how many others you have killed to earn that despicable name."

Thomas laughed. "Nice one. You don't give up, do you?" Thomas replied. "Listen, man, you might as well move on, 'cause what you talkin' 'bout ain't got a damn thang to do wit' who killed Mrs. B., and I didn't do it."

Just then, a uniformed officer came inside the interrogation room and approached Detective Prator, whispering into his ear. Prator then nudged McCaney and gestured him to the hallway.

"A man ran a red light," the uniformed officer began.

"I ain't on traffic no more. Why the fuck you telling me this shit?" McCaney asked.

The uniformed officer looked at McCaney without answering and continued, "He was driving under the influence of alcohol, and not only did the arresting officer find a cigarillo filled with marijuana in the ashtray, but he also found a .44 Magnum."

Prator and McCaney looked one another.

"Interested now?" asked the officer.

"Yeah, yeah. What else you got?" Prator asked.

"The gun is registered to Harvey Sims."

"Any relation to Anna Sims?' McCaney asked.

The uniformed officer walked away. "You want me to do everything for you?"

The detectives went back in the interrogation room.

"You're free to go for now, Killa. But understand that I got my eyes on you," McCaney said. "And pull your pants up, nigga, before I get those south side boys to beat your ass again."

"Yeah, whatever."

# Chapter 38

## *Harvey Sims*

Harvey Sims was processed and placed in an interrogation room to wait for Detectives Prator and McCaney. The .44 Magnum was sent to the lab to see if the bullets matched bullets from the crime scene or any other unsolved murders.

"Harvey Sims," Prator said when he and his partner walked in the room. "You have a big problem, my friend, running a red light, driving under the influence of alcohol."

"Shame on you," McCaney said and laughed a little. "And to make matters worse, you had a cigar filled with weed: a blunt, as you folks call it nowadays. And on top of that, you were carrying a loaded, concealed weapon. What you got to say about all that, my friend?" McCaney then sat down at the table across from Sims.

Sims's only response was, "I ain't sayin' nuttin' 'til I talk wit' a lawyer."

"Just like that, huh?" McCaney said.

Prator sat down at the table next to Sims. "What did you do that you wanna lawyer up right away?"

Once again, Sims's only response was, "I ain't sayin' nuttin' 'til I talk wit' a lawyer."

"Have it your way, Sims, but talking to us now will make it go a lot easier on you in the long run," Prator said and stood up.

"I ain't sayin' nuttin' 'til I talk wit' a lawyer," Sims said again to the detectives and dropped his head. Mc-Caney got up and followed Prator out of the room.

Due to countless unsolved murders in Compton and Los Angeles County, the lab had not completed the necessary work, despite Prator's push for urgency.

Running a red light, driving under the influence of alcohol, a cigar filled with marijuana, and carrying a loaded, concealed weapon, was not enough to satisfy the detective's appetite, but judging by the way Sims lawyered up right away, Prator knew that there was a lot more to this than just traffic, weapon, and weed charges.

"Maybe we were focusing on the wrong person," Prator modestly said to McCaney, who was still so fixated on Daryl Bradford he wasn't trying to hear about anyone else being a potential suspect.

"Maybe, maybe not," McCaney answered. "We won't know nothin' until the lab work gets back."

"Right, but in the meantime, what we need to know is who this guy is; where he works, where he lives, who he's fuckin', his taxes, bank account statements, the whole nine yards. I need to know. It's something about him, Mac, I'm tellin' you it is. My gut tells me there is something about this cat."

"Maybe, maybe not," McCaney said. "One thing is for sure."

"What's that?"

"If he didn't have anything to hide, he would at least talk to us without insisting on the presence of a lawyer."

"Let's try to squeeze an alibi out of him for the night of the murder."

"I was thinkin' the same thing," McCaney said, after giving the scenario a dose of rational thinking.

Prator raised an eyebrow. "You thinking what I'm thinking?" he asked.

"Jumping to conclusions is what got us in this twisted-up shit we in now," McCaney admitted. "I'll tell you what; let's leave that uncooperative piece of shit in that cold-ass room for a few hours or maybe even a day or two, and maybe after sleepin' on that cold-ass cement floor, he'll be ready to talk."

Prator didn't like his partner's cruel and illegal idea. "That's similar to torture, Mac, we can't do that. He said he wants to talk to a lawyer, so—"

McCaney snapped and cut him off. "People in hell want ice water, too! I'm tellin' you, Prator, we gotta do what we gotta do if we ever plan to get to the bottom of this shit!"

"But we've gotta do it right to make it stick." As usual, Prator tried avoiding confrontation with his hot-tempered partner. "Listen, Mac. Just suppose this is really our guy and he killed April Bradford."

"Why would he? He probably don't even know her."

"You know anything else to try?"

"That'll be like using a tree branch to fish in the fuckin' Pacific Ocean."

"Listen, Mac. We've fucked up enough in the past, and—"

McCaney angrily cut him off. "So you blamin' all the fuckups on me? You blamin' the Bradford case on me, too, ain't you?" he asked, getting in Prator's face.

"No, I'm not saying that. Listen, I need you to calm yourself down and brainstorm with me a little, and focus on suspects, facts, and motive, beginning at square one, and for the moment, setting aside Harvey Sims."

"Go ahead and lead."

"Daryl Bradford, we can't say for certain killed his wife, especially after that performance he put on with his lawyer."

"Okay, keep goin'."

"Who else had motive?"

"Anna," McCaney quickly replied. "She could've wanted April dead to make things easier for her to get Daryl to herself."

"Let's consider that, but actually, I think she's too dumb to orchestrate something of that degree."

"No shit. I don't know what Bradford see in her," McCaney said and both men laughed. "Who else would have motive?"

"Anyway, what about Tyrone Whitsey?"

"Why?" McCaney asked, smiling, figuring his partner was on to something worthy.

"Maybe he got mad at April because she told him that she was going to tell Daryl about their affair and soon-to-be baby. How 'bout that?"

"You're on point, and I'm lovin' it."

"Now I see where you going with this, potna."

"Okay, but how stupid do we look, after all this time we been focusing on Daryl Bradford and now, after we arrest him, we on somebody else?"

"It's not about how stupid we look, McCaney, it's about finding out who is actually responsible for killing April Bradford. Listen, man, just because we're detectives doesn't mean we're perfect and don't make mistakes; we're human, and I promise you that both of us will make an incalculable amount of mistakes 'til the day we leave this earth and meet our Maker."

"So what do we do from here?" McCaney asked, embracing his partner's logic.

Just then, an officer handed Prator a piece of paper.

"Check this out, Mac," Prator said and handed McCaney the paper.

"This puts the case in a whole different light."

"It does, doesn't it? So let's began by bringing in Tyrone Whitsey and re-interviewing him."

"I'll get a uniform to have him picked up."

"Good, that's a start. In the interest of stalling for time, we'll hold Harvey Sims on the two bench warrants and gun charge to keep him in custody until the lab reports get back, which will give us time to dig into his history. He's definitely hiding something," Prator said. "I can feel it."

McCaney added his two cents. "He looks like a softie tryin' to be hard. If that's true, he'll break like a pretzel, just give him time." A sudden thought popped in McCaney's mind, causing him to frown and speak out. "All this shit sounds good, Prator, but what about all those inconsistencies in Bradford's story?"

"None of that matters now, Mac, and overall, inconsistencies don't mean he killed his wife. Call Davis and tell him a uniform will be there shortly to pick him up."

"Got it. I'm on it then, boss."

"Don't call me that. How many times I got to tell you that, Mac? Either call me by my name or call me partner, not boss."

"Got it."

# Chapter 39

## *For the Insurance Money*

Tyrone Whitsey arrived at the station at ten minutes to four, and was taken to an interrogation room to wait. He wasn't prepared for the attack Prator and McCaney unleashed on him.

"You lyin' piece of shit!" McCaney screamed, hovering over Tyrone, reading the faxes sent by Mrs. Mitchell.

"What you talkin' 'bout, man?" Tyrone asked. He appeared perplexed and dumbfounded, but the detectives weren't buying it. They'd already seen enough amateur acting performed by Daryl Bradford.

Prator slammed a folder on the table in front of Tyrone. "Why did you keep the insurance policy from us, Davis? And don't lie and say you didn't know about it!"

"Man, what insurance policy y'all talkin' 'bout? I don't know nothin' about no got-damn insurance policy. I ain't neva' paid no kinda insurance in my life and I know my mama ain't took out none on me, so what da hell y'all talkin' 'bout?"

"So you wanna play stupid on us, huh?" McCaney said, snatching Tyrone from his chair and grabbing his shirt collar. Prator observed cautiously, so as not to let his buddy go too far.

"Mac, calm down."

McCaney ignored his partner. "Listen, punk," Mc-Caney said, holding a firm grip on Tyrone's collar. "I couldn't care less that you fucked your best friend's wife, got her pregnant, and in return made off with a cool million dollars, but what I ain't gon' stand for is—"

Tyrone cut him off, mustering a barely audible weep. "A million what?" he whispered.

McCaney slung him against the wall, then clinched his fist and cocked his arm, about to land a knockout blow, until Prator grabbed him.

"I got this," Prator said. "Calm down, partner, calm down." Prator then turned his attention to Tyrone, who'd seated himself. "Open the got-damn folder, Davis," Prator instructed. "If you try to play on our intelligence, I'll walk right outta here and let my partner take over."

"Y'all know damn well I can't read so why y'all fuckin' wit' me? What's dis about a million dollars? Why don't one-a y'all read it to me?"

McCaney nodded in disgust. "Uneducated, stupid, and don't have a bit of damn common sense. You the kinda man who thinks with his dick," McCaney said.

Prator took the liberty of reading first the contents of the letter from April, which read:

Apparently, honey, something unfortunate and tragic has happened to me, which led you to open this letter. I'd like to begin by saying I love you and thank you for all the good times, smiles, and hope you brought me. Remember the day, honey, when I asked you if you would mind taking care of our baby in the event that something happened to me? Well, I guess it's time for you to step up to the plate and become responsible. It's in you to do the right thing, I saw that in you, but obviously opportunity never presented itself. I have a great deal of confidence in you, Tyrone.

McCaney nodded and mumbled derogatory comments toward Tyrone.

Prator continued.

I fell in love with you, Tyrone, because you were everything to me that my husband wasn't. You did things to me and for me that he didn't. It's not always the big things people do for you that count; sometimes the small, thoughtful, and hearty things outweigh expensive things. Thank you for all those days and nights you listened to me complain about Daryl and thank you for giving me constructive advice about certain things and for caring about me in a way that my husband didn't. Your touch, the way you touched me, ump, ump, ump, now I can only long for it. Maybe, just maybe, once you make it up here, we'll reunite. LOL.

Anyhow, thank you for not criticizing me about my issues, and thank you for taking your time and teaching me the full pleasures of sex. Thank you for all those nights we spent staying up late, playing dominoes and spades, listening to oldies but goodies, and making small talk while my husband was out with his other woman. I love you, Tyrone, and I know you loved me too. It wasn't just a sex thing between us; our feelings went far deeper.

Moving on, my father always told me that a million dollars should last the average person a lifetime if it is used wisely. I'm asking you, honey, to use this wisely and to make sure our child wants for nothing. I'm hoping that he is okay and survived whatever devastation I encountered. I'd give my life in a second for our baby to have their shot at life. I love you, Tyrone. And again, thank you for being my bridge over troubled waters.

Another thing my father always told me, which reminds me so much of you; he said that positions or possessions have nothin' to do with a person's heart, meaning that a wealthy person can be hateful and deceptive and a poor person may possess a heart of gold. You possess a heart of gold, honey. I don't regret anything that happened. Until we meet again in heaven, take care, honey. I wish you blessings, peace, prosperity, and good health. Promise me that you will one day tell our child the truth about how it was conceived. One thing I adored about you was that you may have been uneducated, but you still had a keen way of putting things, where a person couldn't help but understand. As my dad always said, put it where the goats can get it. LOL. I love you, honey; kiss the baby for me.

Sincerely,

Your New Love

Tyrone had begun sobbing after hearing the first sentence.

April had taken out an additional insurance policy with an insurance company other than her primary insurance company, for $1 million, and had named Tyrone Whitsey the beneficiary.

McCaney got in Tyrone's face and voiced his view of the scenario. "Now everything is startin' to make sense to me," McCaney said.

Tyrone sat silently, high off April's words, not giving the detectives any regard. "She loved me," Tyrone whimpered. "And I loved her too. She was my girl, man, and she was havin' my baby." He cried, "Why did dat fool have to go and kill her? I hate dat muthafucka, I hate him!"

Just then there was a knock at the door. Another detective stuck his head in and signaled for McCaney.

"What's up, Mac? I need to interrogate a suspect and you guy are hogging all the rooms," the detective said.

"We're not finished with the guy in two. We were waiting to get some results from the lab before we put him in a cage." McCaney leaned forward and whispered, "He lawyered up."

Prator walked out and joined them. "Take our boy and cuff him to that bench out there and get a uniform to watch him," Prator said and turned his attention back to Tyrone.

Over the several days of the case, Prator had meticulously studied Tyrone's demeanor. He detected a level of sincerity, but knew that McCaney was convinced that the man, who'd backstabbed a friend who allowed him to move into his home when he had nowhere else to go or to turn to, was doing nothing more than performing a well-rehearsed act. He had learned to trust his partner's instincts and decided to let him take the lead.

Prator gave McCaney the nod and he stepped up and got in Tyrone's face.

"You fucked your friend's wife," McCaney said. "Then you killed her when you found out she took out that insurance policy! You wanted it all for yourself, didn't you, Davis? A poor, uneducated muthafucka from the ghetto havin' a shot at a mill; you don't fool me, Davis! I can see straight through your conniving, backstabbin' ass! You proved you wasn't shit when you—"

Tyrone cut him off, and stood. "You don't know what da fuck you talkin' about, man! I loved April and would never even think about doin' anything to hurt her. Daryl killed her, and you know he did, but now you wanna try ta twist shit up, like I killed her! Fuck you and fuck what you goin' through!"

"Sit your ass down before I knock you down, punk!" McCaney demanded, face to face with Tyrone.

"Y'all trippin' if y'all think I killed April for some got-damn money," Tyrone insisted. "I been broke all my damn life. I don't give a shit about no got-damn money! You can't miss nothin' you ain't neva' had!

Fuck some money and fuck y'all, too! I'd rather have April any day over a funky-ass million dollars! Fuck what y'all goin' through!"

Prator jumped in. "So are you telling us that you had no knowledge of the insurance policy?"

"Listen, man; I might not know how to read or write, but didn't y'all just hear da letter she wrote? I don't know how either one-a y'all passed a damn test to be a got-damn detective. Guess somebody gave y'all all da fuckin' answers."

McCaney took a step toward Tyrone and again Prator held him back. "You illiterate, backstabbing piece of shit, I should—"

Prator struggled to contain his fuming partner. "Calm down, Mac, calm the fuck down! You can't think when you're mad, and I need your brains right now, so calm down, will you?"

Tyrone Whitsey, in Prator's professional opinion, had no knowledge of the insurance policy, in spite of what his hothead partner thought. The behavior science classes he had taken years earlier helped mold a new thought; a thought he regretted entertaining years earlier.

"Davis," Prator said, reaching in his pocket and pulling out two dollars. "Here, take this and go buy yourself a soda or something from the vending machines down the hall to cool yourself off a little."

Tyrone accepted the money and added his two cents. "I'll pay you back one day, but in da meantime, you need ta cool off dat loose-cannon partner of yours because he's damn sho on da wrong track. Now I see why April's killer ain't locked up."

McCaney snapped again. "Shut the fuck up, punk, and get outta here!"

As Tyrone made his way to the vending machines, he glanced at the man who was handcuffed to the bench and paused when he noticed a familiar face. Tyrone went and got a soda and then came and sat down next to the man.

"What's up, man?" Tyrone said. "Remember me, man?"

"No, now get outta here," Harvey Sims said in almost a whisper.

"Remember we was playin' one-on-one at Wilson Park that day and I beat you by six points?" Tyrone said, smiling.

Harvey looked at Tyrone without answering. He glanced over at the uniformed officer who was watching him. He was reading the paper and eating a jelly doughnut.

"Yeah, man," Tyrone continued, even though it was obvious that Harvey didn't want to talk to him. "You thought I was a ruddy-poop, didn't you?" Tyrone laughed and took a sip of his strawberry soda. "But I busted your bubble, man. Sheeeet; I'm tellin' you man, I'm like Magic Johnson, Kobe Bryant, Kareem Abdul Jabbar, LeBron James, and Michael Jordan, and Derrick Rose combined together, nigga. I'm all dat and some. If you don't know, now you know, nigga," Tyrone said, and busted out in laughter.

Hearing Davis talking, and more importantly, not coming back to the room to finish their conversation, Prator and McCaney stepped out of the interrogation room.

When Harvey saw the detectives come out, he tried his best to ignore Tyrone, but it was impossible. He gestured for him to "shut the fuck up and leave," but unfortunately for him, Tyrone didn't get it.

"They got you too, huh?" Tyrone continued. "Remember when I showed you dat naked chick on my cell phone and told you da fool I was livin' wit' was hittin' it? And remember I told you he was always talkin' shit to me and talkin' down and foul to me, 'cause I didn't have a damn job; remember dat?"

"Get the fuck away from me," Harvey said softly, trying not to be heard by the detectives, but Tyrone just kept on talking like he didn't hear him.

"Remember you asked me where he worked and I told you he worked at da post office? Remember dat, man?"

Now Harvey was openly gesturing for Tyrone to leave, but that never happened.

"Why you playin' like you don't know me, homie?" Tyrone continued. "Hell, I might be able ta help you outta da shit you in, thanks to my girl. From what I understand, I'm a millionaire, homie. Money ain't a thang no mo', you feel me. Man, I'm 'bout ta go get drunk as a muthafucka and celebrate, my nigga. Like Jay-Z said, 'Money Ain't A Thang.'"

Prator and McCaney curiously and slowly approached their loudmouth suspect.

"You know that guy?" Prator asked, raising an eyebrow.

"I don't know 'im personally, but we shot da shit one day at Wilson Park while shootin' hoops, know what I'm sayin'? I took dat fool straight to da hoop and dogged his ass, though. He couldn't hang wit' my skills, jus' like a whole lotta people can't. Some people got it, and some people don't, feel me? Y'all got 'im fo' some bogus bullshit too?"

McCaney took over. "Never mind what we got him for. Your ass ain't off the hook yet, so worry about yourself. Now tell us, what did y'all talk about that day? Did he tell you where he work? I heard you sayin' somethin' about a picture you showed him of a naked chick, and a fool who was always talkin' down to you; why don't you expound on that for us?"

"Expound? What da hell do dat mean?"

"Talk about it, you damn fool, that's what it means. Now tell us what did you two talk about that day," Mc-Caney insisted, getting heated.

Harvey dropped his head, knowing that loose lips sink ships and that his ship, by the looks of Tyrone's lips constantly moving, was about to sink.

Tyrone showed the detectives five pictures of Anna posing naked. Prator and McCaney looked at each other, then they both looked at Harvey, who had dropped his head.

"Where did you get these pictures, Tyrone?" Prator asked.

"One day Daryl was bragging about how fine dis chick he was fuckin' was and how good she was sexually. Then he sent these pictures to my cell phone, and I jus' neva' deleted 'em."

The woman in the picture was Anna Sims and she appeared as happy as could be in each pose, smiling, while showing off her assets, and enjoying every second of it. She held her vagina open on one pose, and sucked on a huge, black dildo on another pose. The next was a shot of her sitting on the dildo. In another flick she licked her left nipple, and in another one she was bent over as if she were hiking a football, holding open her butthole.

"Have a seat, Davis," Prator said.

"We'll get back to you in a minute," McCaney said and unlocked Harvey's handcuffs. McCaney stood him up and dragged Harvey in the interrogation room.

"You wanna tell us about this, Sims?" Prator asked.

"Or do you still want to wait on the court-appointed lawyer to get here?" McCaney added.

Prator sat down next to Sims. "I can guarantee that it will go a lot better for you at this point if you talk to us now," Prator said.

"Harvey Sims," McCaney said. "Anna Sims was your wife, wasn't she?"

Harvey nodded his head, and thought about what the detectives had just told him. He knew once they tested his gun that he would need to cut a deal.

"You killed April Bradford, didn't you?" Prator said.

"You were mad 'cause the clown Bradford was fuckin' your wife," McCaney said.

"She probably left him for Bradford," Prator added.

"Shit, I can understand that. The man fuckin' your wife, and took her from you," McCaney said in his most sympathetic voice. He patted Harvey on the shoulder.

"What happened, Harvey? Did you go over there that night looking for Bradford and found the wife instead?"

"Did you think about getting you some in the shower? McCaney asked. "Talk to us, man. We can make this go a whole lot easier on you."

"What went thought your mind when some guy you're playing ball with showed you naked pictures of your wife?" Prator asked.

"That day at Wilson Park," Harvey began slowly, "I was furious seeing my wife on that nigga's phone, posing like she some kinda cheap slut. Like she was aimin' to get a porn movie deal. I did the best I could not to let him see how mad I really was. I didn't want that nigga to know that the woman on the pictures was my wife."

"You still loved her," Prator said. "Even though you and her had been separated for years."

"Yeah, I still loved her. And even though we hadn't have sex for months before the separation, because she was having sex with Daryl, I refused to let go and accept the fact that she no longer wanted me."

While the detectives asked questions, Harvey's mind drifted off to a conversation he had with Anna, the day she told him that it was over between them.

*"If I can't have you, can't nobody have you! Do you understand that? I'll kill a muthafucka over you, don't you know that by now, Anna?"*

*"Please, Harvey, why it gotta be about all that?"*

*"I took care of you when you didn't have a damn thing; not a pot to piss in or a window to throw it out of! Bitch."*

*"You don't have to call me a bitch."*

*"I paid for you to go to cosmetology school, but you dropped out halfway through the got-damn course! I fed you, put a roof over your head, bought you whatever the hell you wanted, made sure you always had money, and this is the thanks I get, bitch? Oh, hell no, I don't think so! If I can't have you, nobody can have you, and I mean that! Bitch, you bought and paid for, remember that!" he told Anna and stormed out of the house.*

Even though the lab had worked overtime to obtain the results on the .44 Magnum, eleven hours after interrogating Harvey Sims, the results had finally come back, matching the bullets that killed April Bradford.

In a no-win situation, being confronted with undeniable, concrete evidence, Harvey Sims confessed to killing April Bradford for a reason that made sense only to him, saying, "Her husband took something of mines, so I took something of his! I just wanted to take something, something like a wife from him. Damn right I did it and I'd do it again if it came down to it! I made that bitch get on her knees in the bathtub and beg me for her life, but that crazy-ass Jesus freak turned away from me and started prayin', speakin' in tongues and shit! I guess she thought that was gon' stop me from blowin' her brains out! I shot her three times in the got-damn head and like I said, I'd do it again if I had to! You take from me, I'll get you back where it hurts! Payback is a muthafucka! And as far as Anna goes, she mighta been his woman, but I still had papers on the slut bitch, and she was my got-damn wife!"

The confession was good and all to the detectives, but McCaney was still puzzled about something.

"How did you get past that vicious dog?"

"Easy. Just threw 'im two poisoned steaks. It took a little while, but he began to get weaker and weaker, and within seconds his barks became whimpers. Then he slumped to the ground. The poison wasn't gonna kill him, but it would put him down long enough for me to handle my business."

# Chapter 40

## *Whoops, We Were on the Wrong Damn Track All Along*

They sipped Hennessy at Prator's condo, which he utilized as his playhouse.

"This is my 'I need to get the hell away from my wife for a while' spot," Prator bragged.

He had purchased the property years earlier. In the beginning he planned to surprise his wife one day and take her to see it, but changed his mind after a night of fun and pleasure with an expensive hooker. Secretly, he had borrowed from his 401(k).

"Home away from home and away from my nagging-ass wife," Prator said to McCaney. "This is where I exhale and relax, my friend, setting aside police work, issues, stressful cases, and like I said, a break from my wife." He busted out in laughter.

McCaney chuckled, nodding, while saying something sarcastic as usual. "Smart, but yet so dumb," McCaney said. "I'm gon' tell you somethin', man; you actually think your wife don't know you out here fuckin' around? Nigga, please."

"Not unless you told her. No one knows about it but you and the call girls who've been here."

"Like I said, man; smart but yet so dumb."

Prator took a sip of Henny. "First of all, Mr. Know-it-all, my wife isn't like Anna Sims, or bold as April

Bradford; and secondly, she's a church woman, filled with the Holy Ghost."

McCaney laughed so hard he almost choked on his drink. "Let me tell you somethin', playa," he said, still laughing. "Women know when their men are fuckin' other women, trust me, potna. They just don't say nothin' about it. They'll let you have enough rope to hang yourself. You see, man, most time men die before their wives do.

"In fact, let me tell you about my Uncle Leroy. Uncle Leroy is a contractor and a part-time preacher at a small church, who makes boatloads of cash, but tricks it off on women. Uncle Leroy owned five houses his wife knew about, and another house, which he calls his playhouse, that he thinks his wife don't know about, but in secret she does know about it, but she don't let him know she know. He thinks he's doing something slick, but he ain't.

"Uncle Leroy is what I call a male ho, without a conscience. He fucked his best friend's wife, knowing his friend was at work, he fucked his brother's ol' lady, and he got three or four bitches he fucks at his so-called 'playhouse,' and what gets me, man, is that the muthafucka is at church every Sunday morning, preaching the Word of God! He is so bold, his fave, short for favorite, is right there in church with him and his wife damn near every Sunday! But he's like you, and thinks his wife don't know! Don't be no damn fool, man. A wife will let you go out there and do what the hell you wanna do, like buy a secret house, and other shit, and she'll wait for your stupid, slick ass to kick the bucket and all that shit will be hers! Man, you remind me so much of my Uncle Leroy."

Prator listened, but fired back when McCaney had finished. "Fuck you and Uncle Leroy! I'm my own man, you understand?"

McCaney chuckled. "Yeah, I heard that. Tell me somethin', slick, when was the last time you fuc . . . Whoops, my bad. I mean, when was the last time you made love to your wife?"

Prator jumped on the offensive. "What kinda question is that to ask another man?"

"The kinda question most men like you don't wanna answer. I bet you ain't even hittin' it no more, are you? That's what I'm talkin' about; that's the main sign, dummy. Anytime a man stop fuckin' his woman, don't you think she'll begin to get suspicious?"

"Whatever, man. Like I said, you think you know every got-damn thing, Mr. Know-it-all. And the thing about you is that you're not even married."

"That's my prerogative. Been there, done that. But I'll tell you what; I fuck a whole lot of married women. In fact, all that shit about your wife is a church woman . . . Let me tell you somethin' about church women, potna: their pussies get hot too, and they like to fuck just like ungodly woman like to fuck. Hell, some of them are even freakier than the average freaky women.

"Check this out, man; I've been fuckin' three church women for three years, and guess what? All of 'em are married. How 'bout that? I met 'em at church, because that's what I do. I go to church to single out the fine, lonely ones, and before you know it, I'm beatin' up that pussy, and I mean beatin' it up good.

"And the good thing about married women is that after you're done fuckin' their brains out, you can send 'em back to their husbands. And most of 'em don't ask me for a got-damn thing. All they want is to be dicked down in a real way. I dick 'em down on Saturday, and Sunday mornin' they at church singin' and clappin', dancin' and shoutin' out praises, so, man, don't tell me shit about church women!

"And oh, don't forget about that old song by Johnnie Taylor: 'Who's makin' love to your old lady while you are out makin' love?' And also remember what Tyrone says that April said: when vows are broken shit happens. Listen, potna, sometimes it's okay to be a fool, once, but, man, just don't be a damn fool! You with me?"

Prator was agitated by McCaney's logic and examples, causing him to nod disapprovingly and frown. His tone signified his annoyance. "You finished, man?" Prator asked.

McCaney laughed. "I didn't strike a nerve, did I?"

"Fuck you."

"Can't handle the truth, huh? Don't trip, but I'm just getting started," McCaney said. "Answer me this question, Prator: why is it that most men can't handle when their wives fuck around on them, but expect their wives to forgive them when they get caught fuckin' around? Now what if you walked in, at your own home, one day and found your wife naked, sittin' between two long, big-dick men, with one in each hand, just havin' the time of her life? You would hit the ceiling, wouldn't you? But if your wife walked in on you and one of your call girls, you'd be sayin' some shit like, 'Baby, I can explain.' No offense, man, I'm just tryin' to put you up on game, potna, that's it and that's all. Never think your game is so tight you can't get played." He laughed loudly.

Prator was on fire. "Kiss my ass, Mac," Prator angrily replied. "You say some of the most stupidest shit! I can't believe that shit came out of your mouth."

"I'm just keepin' it real, man. That's why I'm single," McCaney added.

Having heard enough of his partner's cynicism and sarcasm, Prator changed subjects. "Man, the Bradford case was a whirlpool of shit and surprises, wasn't it?"

"Yep, it damn sho was. I was thinkin' about it earlier; the reality of the scenario was that Bradford was cheatin' on his wife with Anna Sims, who was cheatin' on her husband, Harvey. And then you have the broke, long-dick, pretty-boy, ghetto-fabulous, smooth-talkin' Tyrone who swerved in like a snake, fucks his best friend's woman who he sense ain't gettin' dicked down by her husband, and takes advantage of a golden opportunity and came out of it a millionaire. Ain't that some shit?"

"Yep," Prator replied. "Enough to write a book about or make a movie out of it."

"It shoulda been me," McCaney said, nodding. "Some guys have all the luck, some guys get all the breaks." He took another sip of Hennessy, thinking deeply about his ex-wife, who'd cheated on him, which triggered him to initiate a fast divorce.

Prator continued, as McCaney's mind continued to drift. "The part I liked about it was the confession," Prator said. "Harvey Sims said he outright told Anna that if he couldn't have her, then nobody could have her. But what I really don't get is that he hadn't fucked her in years. Why was he still so obsessed behind her?"

"Pussy," McCaney said, snapping back to reality. "Some women can put it on you so damn good, you'll find yourself obsessed over her. That kinda shit happens every day, and not only that; I see it in the movies all the time. Yeah, man, that was some weird shit, wasn't it?"

"And poor Daryl Bradford; we sent him through the shit-wringer, didn't we?"

"Fuck him, and that illiterate, ghetto-feet muthafucka, Tyrone," McCaney said, frowning. "I don't like narcissistic pieces of shit like them! People like Daryl

think that everyday rules don't apply to him, just because he served in the got-damn military! He's an egotistical punk, who thinks he can treat people and talk to
people any kinda way he wants, because he's convinced
he's better than them or special. Man, I wanted to bust
his ass up on GP. And while we're on the subject of
Bradford, somethin' all you married men need to keep
in mind."

"What's that?" Prator asked, giving his partner a
stern look.

"What goes around comes around twice as hard.
Don't you believe in karma?"

"Kinda sorta.'"

"You best believe in it. I'm tellin' you, it's real shit,
man."

"You got that shit right," Prator agreed, but didn't
read between the lines.

"You didn't get the message in my comment, did you,
partner?" McCaney asked, snickering.

Prator silenced himself a few moments, scratching
his head, and then gave McCaney the middle finger.
"Fuck you."

"No offense, potna, but think about it," McCaney
said, now laughing. "She might be your wife, but at the
same time another man could be rockin' her world sexually, and makin' her call him daddy in the process."

"Kiss my ass, McCaney."

"I'm just sayin', man, that's real talk. That's why I'm
single. I fuck who I wanna fuck, includin' wives, church
women, et cetera. I slang this soul-pole in whoever I
want."

"Whatever, man," Prator said, then added, "We both
know why you're single."

McCaney shot a disapproving look at his partner.
"You can't leave what's in the past buried, can you?"

"I can, but you keep throwin' darts at me," Prator said, laughing. "That was some bold shit you did, man, I swear it was. Sometimes I bust out laughing, thinking about it while driving, at my desk, and a few times I thought about it when I was taking a shit and busted up on the toilet. People thought I was crazy, man, but only if they knew what I was laughing about. You had a ton of nerves to call the husband of the woman you was fuckin', tell him how good his wife's pussy and head was, and how she pulled your dick outta her pussy before you came, and sucked it dry." Prator laughed even louder. "That was some bold shit, man."

McCaney took another sip. "Yeah, I fucked up on that one. I was really just tryin' to pay my wife back for cheatin' on me, but I was just in too deep and got caught up. Goes to show you that two wrongs don't make a right. But what really fucked me up about that was that I had been faithful to Alise. Man, I had never even thought about cheatin' on her. We had been together since junior high school, and like I said, I had never even thought about cheatin' on her. And check this shit out, man. She said she cheatin' on me because I wasn't givin' her the attention she felt she deserved."

"The same reason April cheated on Daryl, right?" Prator said.

"Right. Man, I guess women really down with that 'attention' shit, you know? But anyway, she said that I was always so caught up chasing a suspect, or obsessed with a case, that I gave her no attention, so apparently she found a muthafucka who gave her that desired attention. Yeah, when I found out, she didn't lie about it, and told me why she did it. So I tried paying her back by fucking this chick, Celeste, who'd been throwing her pussy at me left and right, for a few years, and I got caught up. The trust factor between me and Alise was gone. I didn't trust her and she didn't trust me, so we decided to get a divorce."

"So are you still fucking Celeste?" Prator asked.

"I hit it every now and then, that's about it.""

"So do you ever plan on getting married again?"

"To tell you the truth, I ain't gave it any thought." He developed a frown and continued with an attitude. "You see, Prator, it's muthafuckas like you who cheat on their good wives and shit, and make it hard for faithful men in the world like me. That's another reason why I was always so mad with Bradford; I thought he had cheated on his wife, like you be doing, which caused her to cheat with Tyrone. I don't like that shit, man. A man is s'posed to treat his wife like golden, you know. A good wife is something to cherish, to love, and be committed to. Your s'posed to treat them special, like you would treat your own mother. I don't like all that cheating and shit, man. Yeah, I enjoy being single and fucking who I wanna fuck, driving my expensive cars, owning a big, pretty house and shit, having plenty of money, but the truth of the matter is that I get lonely sometimes, you know? I get lonely as hell sometimes, man. I sit in my luxurious home, all alone. I drive my Lex or my Vette, all alone. No one to watch a good Tyler Perry play or movie with, no one to cook me a good home-cooked meal, no one to hug or give a meaningful kiss to; man, that shit fucks with me sometimes, I ain't gonna lie about it. But that's the kinda shit that happens when vows are broken. You can bet your ass that when I do run across a good woman, or she runs across me, I'm damn sure gonna know how to appreciate and treat her."

Prator really didn't appreciate McCaney's candor and word choice, but shrugged it off and continued to be sociable and pleasant. "So what are you gonna do about it?" Prator asked with a concerned ear. "You mean that out of all the women in your stable, none of them are wifey material?"

"To tell you the truth, Celeste digs the hell outta me, man. Hell, she's about the only one who likes me for me, and not for what I've got. She's a simple woman, you know, not all that high maintenance shit; new wigs every goddamn two weeks, nails and feet did once a goddamn month, and what I really like about her is that she don't wear all that clown-shit, makeup and shit. Man, I can't stand a woman who wears all that shit. You know, the only thing about her is that she's kinda unattractive and a little on the heavy side. But other than that, she's—"

Prator cut him off. "Are you fucking kidding me? When are you gonna learn that beauty comes from within? Man, all that beauty and ass fades away with age. You'd better be looking for someone who has your back to grow old with, instead of a fine-ass woman who just might leave your ass at home when you're sick and not only go out and gamble your money at the casino, but will take another man along with her and pay his way with your money, driving your got-damn car. You better wake up, man!"

"Man, I just wish Alise wouldn'ta cheated on me," McCaney said, then took another sip.

"That's in the past. Live for today, next week, next month, and ten years from now. Leave the past behind," Prator advised. "Five years from now, the way you're going, you'll still be saying the same old shit about, 'Man, I wish Alise woulda just done right and not cheated.'"

McCaney frowned. "You mocking me, man?"

"I ain't mocking you, I'm just saying."

After a few moments of silence, McCaney spoke out. "Yeah, man, it might be me and Celeste one day, who knows. She's the only one I trust, you know?"

"How long you been knowing her?"

"A few years now. If there ever happens to be a wedding, you be the first to know." He smiled at the notion.

"Is she a church woman?" Prator asked.

McCaney eyed him suspiciously, not knowing what angle Prator was coming from, assuming his question may have stemmed from his recent comments he'd made about the numerous church woman he'd slept with.

"Yeah, she goes to church, not every Sunday, but she goes. Most time she works on Sundays. She's a nurse."

"Oh, okay."

"Yeah. I'm glad she's doing something with her life other than just throwing it away, doing nothing, and depending on some form of a government check. But you know what, man? It's funny how I know people who aren't Christians and don't go to church at all, but they're good people, and the other hand I know professed Christians who are full of shit, man. They show up at Church every got-damn Sunday, filled with the Holy Ghost, jumpin' up and down and dancing around and shit like that, and as soon as they leave church they engage in all sorts of sinful shit. I hate that kinda shit, man, and I ain't got a problem calling a muthafucka out on it.

"One thing I can't stand is a got-damn hypocrite. Another thing that bothers me sometimes about Celeste— well, maybe not bothers me, but is a concern—is that she's a Christian and, man, you know how I feel about preachers. All they want is your got-damn money! Most of 'em anyway. I can't see myself giving another man a portion of my money to tell me how to get to heaven, when most 'em ain't living right themselves. Lately, I've been studying the Quran, and man, it's deep. To me, Muslims are the real deal, especially when it comes to discipline and faith. I can see myself fitting right into that religion, it fits me. A militant, outspoken man of faith. But, back to the basics, I don't know if a Christian woman and a Muslim man can make it."

Prator nodded his head in disgust. "You ignorant man of little faith," Prator said. "Let me tell you something; my brother is a Jehovah's Witness and his wife is a Christian, and they've been married for thirty-something years, for starters. They've got five kids together, and both of them own separate, successful businesses. The thing about it, Mac, is that respect and understanding comes in to play in a situation like that. He respects her beliefs and religion and she respect his. And I can say that out of all the years they've been together, as far as I know, they have never wavered in love. Love, respect, and understanding are the key elements in that sort of situation."

McCaney smiled. "Damn, man, you're in the wrong career; you shoulda been a counselor."

"Man, you know what; I've got a nephew," McCaney said. "I think he's about twenty-four, twenty-five, something like that. But anyway, he was headed down the wrong path; stealing, hanging out with gang members, called himself a so-called Crip. Been to jail a few times and even to prison once. Anyway, I took him under my wing and tried to get him out of that shit, and help him lead a worthy life, you know. But man, the more I tried, it seemed like the more he chose to engage in bullshit. The only time he would listen and act like he had any got-damn sense is when he was locked up. I guess that was because I was sending him money. In fact, just last week the muthafucka got caught stealing out of Walmart, and because he had so many got-damn priors, they gave his ass five years. Five fuckin' years for stealing some got-damn Alka-Seltzer. Ain't that a bitch! I tried, but, man, I gotta wash my hands of him. But see, I blame that shit on my sister having different niggas in and out of her life, letting her kids see that shit."

"Damn," Prator said, nodding in disgust. "Your sister gets down like that?"

"Both of 'em do," McCaney said. "Man, I can't understand for the life of me why they're always attracted to nothing-ass, jobless men. I don't understand that shit, man. Both of 'em drove my mama straight to her grave. Mama was always worried about her girls, you know. She died of a heart attack about seven years ago, and I'll tell you what, Prator; I blamed it on my sisters and wanted to kill both those bitches for taking Mama through so much unnecessary shit. Worrying trigger stress, and Mama was always stressed out behind one of my sisters. Man, I ain't been right ever since my mama died. I been mad at the whole got-damn world and developed this 'I don't give a fuck' attitude, ever since. They took something from me I loved, you know what I mean, Mac? My mama meant the world to me, I swear she did. I cussed my sisters out after the funeral, and ain't spoken to neither one of 'em since. That's probably why my oldest sister, Shannon, is having all those problems with my nephew."

"Sorry to hear all of that, Mac. Well, what about your father, man?"

"Who? Man, I ain't never saw him before. The muth-afucka found out my mama was pregnant with me and bounced. As far as I'm concerned, wherever he is he can kiss my ass."

"I heard that," Prator said. "That's unfortunate, man."

McCaney, tired of speaking about family members, shifted the conversation back to the Bradford case. "That damn Daryl Bradford shouldn't made me mad and threaten me about what he was gon' do to me when he see me. You know I don't take easy to threats."

"Anyway," Prator said, quickly changing subjects. "Overall, what did you learn from the Bradford case?"

"That people gon' fuck who they wanna fuck."

"Well, that's true, too," Prator agreed. "But what was the real message in that entire Bradford episode?"

"I just told you, man, people—"

Prator cut him off before he could finish. "The way things played out in the Bradford case should have taught both of us to never be judgmental toward anyone, and not to allow perception to compel our decisions; things aren't always what they seem," Prator said.

"You got that shit right; things aren't always what they seem. Everything that glitters ain't gold. And don't leave out 'when vows are broken shit happens.'"

"You can say that again."

"It's funny how you can know someone for years, but don't really know them as good as you think you do."

Prator glared at McCaney, sensing the comment was directed at him.

McCaney chuckled. "You got a guilty conscience, don't you?"

Prator flipped him off, but actually McCaney never even knew it was due to being fixated on the words "things aren't always what they seem." He thought about how wrong he was in his assessment of Daryl Bradford, perceiving him as a wife killer. McCaney despised most military men due to various confrontations with several of them he encountered since being in law enforcement. To him, they all possessed narcissistic mentalities: better than anyone else. McCaney, having never served in the military, didn't like or tolerate their attitudes. In fact, he was 6-and-0 in physical fights with military-background coworkers. He had kicked their asses, giving them memorable and embarrassing ass whippings.

The following week, while still meditating on the words "things aren't always what they seem," planning to use that quote in both life and work situations, McCaney joined the Nation of Islam, and began worshipping at a mosque an hour away from his home. He befriended two Muslim brothers who carefully mentored him during his transformation period. His transformation caused him not only to become a better person and deal with life in general in a different perspective, but it had also enhanced his detective skills. In addition to that, he even stopped wearing hip-hop attire.

He accepted and respected Celeste for who she was, even though his mentors were strongly against him marrying a Christian woman as opposed to marrying a Muslim.

Six months later, McCaney married Celeste, and as promised Prator was his best man.

Nine months later, at age forty-two, McCaney had his first child, a son, who bore the name Donald McCaney Jr. This was also Celeste's first child.

Life had never been better for McCaney, now known in the Nation of Islam as Al-Baqi. The name reflected "The ever enduring and Immutable," in laymen terms meaning, unchallengeable, absolute, and undeniable. McCaney had finally found what he'd been missing for all those years; Allah, his God, and a good, understanding, virtuous woman.

# ORDER FORM
## URBAN BOOKS, LLC
97 N18th Street
Wyandanch, NY 11798

Name:(please print):_____

Address:       _____

City/State:    _____

Zip:           _____

| QTY | TITLES | PRICE |
|-----|--------|-------|
| | 16 On The Block | $14.95 |
| | A Girl From Flint | $14.95 |
| | A Pimp's Life | $14.95 |
| | Baltimore Chronicles | $14.95 |
| | Baltimore Chronicles 2 | $14.95 |
| | Betrayal | $14.95 |
| | Black Diamond | $14.95 |
| | Black Diamond 2 | $14.95 |
| | Black Friday | $14.95 |
| | Both Sides Of The Fence | $14.95 |
| | Both Sides Of The Fence 2 | $14.95 |
| | California Connection | $14.95 |

Shipping and handling-add $3.50 for 1st book, then $1.75 for each additional book.
Please send a check payable to:
**Urban Books, LLC**
Please allow 4-6 weeks for delivery

# ORDER FORM
## URBAN BOOKS, LLC
97 N18th Street
Wyandanch, NY 11798

Name:(please print):_____

Address:         _____

City/State:      _____

Zip:             _____

| QTY | TITLES | PRICE |
|-----|--------|-------|
|  | California Connection 2 | $14.95 |
|  | Cheesecake And Teardrops | $14.95 |
|  | Congratulations | $14.95 |
|  | Crazy In Love | $14.95 |
|  | Cyber Case | $14.95 |
|  | Denim Diaries | $14.95 |
|  | Diary Of A Mad First Lady | $14.95 |
|  | Diary Of A Stalker | $14.95 |
|  | Diary Of A Street Diva | $14.95 |
|  | Diary Of A Young Girl | $14.95 |
|  | Dirty Money | $14.95 |
|  | Dirty To The Grave | $14.95 |

Shipping and handling-add $3.50 for 1st book, then $1.75 for each additional book.

Please send a check payable to:
**Urban Books, LLC**
Please allow 4-6 weeks for delivery

## ORDER FORM
## URBAN BOOKS, LLC
### 97 N18th Street
### Wyandanch, NY 11798

Name:(please print):_____

Address:        _____

City/State:     _____

Zip:            _____

| QTY | TITLES | PRICE |
|-----|--------|-------|
|     | Gunz And Roses | $14.95 |
|     | Happily Ever Now | $14.95 |
|     | Hell Has No Fury | $14.95 |
|     | Hush | $14.95 |
|     | If It Isn't love | $14.95 |
|     | Kiss Kiss Bang Bang | $14.95 |
|     | Last Breath | $14.95 |
|     | Little Black Girl Lost | $14.95 |
|     | Little Black Girl Lost 2 | $14.95 |
|     | Little Black Girl Lost 3 | $14.95 |
|     | Little Black Girl Lost 4 | $14.95 |
|     | Little Black Girl Lost 5 | $14.95 |

Shipping and handling-add $3.50 for 1st book, then $1.75 for each additional book.

Please send a check payable to:

**Urban Books, LLC**

Please allow 4-6 weeks for delivery

ORDER FORM
URBAN BOOKS, LLC
97 N18th Street
Wyandanch, NY 11798

Name: (please print): _____

Address: _____

City/State: _____

Zip: _____

| QTY | TITLES | PRICE |
|-----|--------|-------|
| | | $14.95 |
| | | 14.95 |
| | | 14.95 |
| | | 14.95 |
| | | 4.95 |
| | | 4.95 |
| | | 4.95 |
| | | 4.95 |
| | | 4.95 |
| | | 4.95 |
| | | 4.95 |
| | | 4.95 |

1.75 for